MICHAEL'S MERCY

Heroes for Hire, Book 10
Sleeper SEAL, Book 3

Dale Mayer

Books in This Series:

Books in the SEALs of Honor Series:

Find out who the Commander calls next. Make sure to pick up ALL the books in the Sleeper SEAL series. These can be read in any order and each stands alone.

MICHAEL'S MERCY: HEROES FOR HIRE, BOOK 10
Dale Mayer
Valley Publishing

Copyright © 2017

This is a work of fiction. Names, characters, places, brands, media, and incidents are either the product of the author's imagination or are used fictitiously. Any resemblance to actual events, locales, or persons, living or dead, is entirely coincidental.

ISBN-13: 978-1-773360-33-1
Print Edition

Back Cover

The Sleeper SEALs are former US Navy SEALs recruited by a new CIA counterterrorism division to handle solo dark-op missions to combat terrorism on US soil.

When things go bad in Michael's world, things go horribly, terrifyingly bad.

It's been one year since hardened Navy SEAL Michael Hampton walked away from his career. He never thought to return, but then his former commander called with the news that an old friend was murdered while undercover—and the commander needs Michael's help.

Knowing the next dead body might be his, Michael takes his friend's place at the home of man bankrolling a terrorist cell. Michael's official mission is to find out all he can to bring down the man's operation. Michael's personal mission is to find out who murdered his friend.

Mercy got the maid job that her sister had last held—just before she was murdered. With the police lacking leads and persons-of-interest, Mercy decides it's up to her to find out what happened. Inside the huge home, she meets Michael and becomes immediately suspicious ... and immediately attracted.

When their paths cross, she realizes he's not who he seems either.

Can they each find the truth about their objectives and about themselves? Or will the terrorists' money man get wind of the traitors in his midst and take care of them before they can take care of him?

Each story in this multiauthor-branded series is a standalone novel, and the series can be read in any order.

Welcome to *Michael's Mercy*, Book 10 in the Heroes for Hire series, reconnecting readers with the unforgettable men from SEALs of Honor in a new series of action-packed, page-turning romantic suspense that fans have come to expect from USA TODAY best-selling author Dale Mayer. This book is part of the continuity series Sleeper SEALS (Book 3).

Sign up to be notified of all Dale's releases here!

http://dalemayer.com/category/blog/

Your Free Book Awaits!

KILL OR BE KILLED

Part of an elite SEAL team, Mason takes on the dangerous jobs no one else wants to do – or can do. When he's on a mission, he's focused and dedicated. When he's not, he plays as hard as he fights.

Until he meets a woman he can't have but can't forget. Software developer, Tesla lost her brother in combat and has no intention of getting close to someone else in the military. Determined to save other US soldiers from a similar fate, she's created a program that could save lives. But other countries know about the program, and they won't stop until they get it – and get her.

Time is running out ... For her ... For him ... For them ...

DOWNLOAD a ***complimentary*** copy of MASON? Just tell me where to send it!

http://dalemayer.com/sealsmason/

Prologue

RETIRED NAVY COMMANDER Greg Lambert leaned forward to rake in the pile of chips his full house had netted him. Tonight he would leave the weekly gathering not only with his pockets full, but his pride intact.

The scowls he earned from his poker buddies at his unusual good luck was an added bonus. They'd become too accustomed to him coming up on the losing side of five-card stud. It was about time he taught them to never underestimate him.

Vice President Warren Angelo downed the rest of his bourbon and stubbed out his Cuban cigar. "Looks like Lady Luck is on your side tonight, Commander."

After he neatly stacked his chips in a row at the rail in front of him, Greg glanced around at his friends. It occurred to him right then, this weekly meeting wasn't so different from the joint sessions they used to have at the Pentagon during his last five years of service.

The location was the Secretary of State's basement now, but the gathering still included top ranking military brass, politicians, and the director of the CIA, who had been staring at him strangely all night.

"It's about time the bitch smiled my way, don't you

think? She usually just cleans out my pockets and gives you my money," Greg replied with a sharp laugh as his eyes roved over the spacious man-cave with envy before they snagged on the wall clock.

It was well past midnight, their normal break-up time. He needed to get home, but what did he have to go home to? Four walls and Karen's mean-as-hell Chihuahua who hated him. Greg stood, scooted back his chair and stretched his shoulders. The rest of his poker buddies quickly left, except for Vice President Angelo, Benedict Hughes with the CIA, and their host tonight, Percy Long, the Secretary of State.

He took the last swig of his bourbon, then set the glass on the table. When he took a step to leave, they moved to block his way to the door. "Something on your minds, gentlemen?" he asked, their cold, sober stares making the hair on the back of his neck stand up.

It wasn't a comfortable feeling, but one he was familiar with from his days as a Navy SEAL. That feeling usually didn't portend anything good was about to go down. But neither did the looks on these men's faces.

Warren cleared his throat and leaned against the mahogany bar with its leather trimmings. "There's been a significant amount of chatter lately." He glanced at Ben. "We're concerned."

Greg backed up a few steps, putting some distance between himself and the men. "Why are you telling me this? I've been out of the loop for a while now." Greg was retired, and bored stiff, but not stiff enough to tackle all that was wrong in the United States at the moment or fight the politics involved in fixing things.

Ben let out a harsh breath then gulped down his glass of water. He set the empty glass down on the bar with a sigh and met Greg's eyes. "We need your help, and we're not going to beat around the bush," he said, making Greg's short hairs stand taller.

Greg put his hands in his pockets, rattling the change in his right pocket and his car keys in the left while he waited for the hammer. Nothing in Washington, D.C. was plain and simple anymore. Not that it ever had been.

"Spit it out, Ben," he said, eyeballing the younger man. "I'm all ears."

"Things have changed in the US and terrorists are everywhere now," he started.

Greg bit back a laugh at the understatement of the century. He'd gotten out before the recent INCONUS attacks started, but he was still in service on 9/11 for the ultimate attack. The day that replaced Pearl Harbor as the day that would go down in infamy.

"That's not news, Ben," Greg said, his frustration mounting in his tone. "What does that have to do with me, other than being a concerned citizen?"

"More cells are being identified every day," Ben replied, his five o'clock shadow standing in stark contrast to his now paler face. "The chatter about imminent threats, big jihad events that are in the works, is getting louder every day."

"You do understand I'm no longer active service, right?" Greg shrugged. "I don't see how I can be of much help there."

"We want you to head a new division at the CIA," Warren interjected. "Ghost Ops, a sleeper cell of SEALs to help us combat the terrorist sleeper cells in the US ... and whatever the hell else might pop up later."

Greg laughed. "And where do you think I'll find these SEALs to sign up? Most are deployed over—"

"We want retired SEALs like yourself. We've spent millions training these men and letting them sit idle stateside while we fight this losing battle alone is just a waste." Ben huffed a breath. "I know they'd respect you when you ask them to join the contract team you'd be heading up. You'd have a much better chance of convincing them to help."

"Most of those guys are like me, worn out to the bone or injured when they finally give up the teams. Otherwise, they'd still be active. SEALs don't just quit." Unless their wives were taken by cancer and their kids were off at college, leaving them alone in a rambling house when they were supposed to be traveling together and enjoying life. "What kind of threats are you talking about?" Greg asked, wondering why he was even entertaining such a stupid idea.

"There are many. More every day. Too many for us to fight alone," Ben started, but Warren held up his palm.

"The president is taking a lot of heat. He has three and a half years left in his term, and taking out these threats was a campaign promise. He wants the cells identified and the terror threats eradicated quickly."

These three, and the president, sat behind desks all day. They'd never been on a field op before, so they had no idea the planning and training that took place before a team ever made it to the field. Training a team of broken down SEALs to work together would take double that time because each knew better than the rest how things should be done, so there was no "quick" about it.

"That's a tall order. I can't possibly get a team of twelve men on the same page in under a year. Even if I can find them." Why in the hell was he getting excited then? "Most are probably out enjoying life on a beach somewhere." Exactly where he would be with Karen if she hadn't fucking died on him as soon as he retired four years ago.

"We don't want a team, Greg," Percy Long corrected, unfolding his arms as he stepped toward him. "This has to be done stealthily because we don't want to panic the public. If word got out about the severity of the threats, people wouldn't leave their homes. The press would pump it up until they created a frenzy. You know how that works."

"So let me get this straight. You want individual SEALs, sleeper guys who agree to be called up for special ops, to perform solo missions?" Greg asked, his eyebrows lifting. "That's not usually how they work."

"Unusual times call for unusual methods, Greg. They have the skills to get it done quickly and quietly," Warren replied.

Greg couldn't argue. That's exactly the way SEALs operated—they did whatever it took to get the job done.

Ben approached him, placed his hand on his shoulder as if this was a tag-team effort, and Greg had no doubt that it was just that. "Every terrorist or wanna-be terror organization has roots here now. Al Qaeda, The Muslim Brotherhood, Isis or the Taliban—you name it. They're not here looking for asylum. They're actively recruiting followers and planning events to create a caliphate on our home turf. We can't let that happen, Greg, or the United States will never be the same."

"You'll be a CIA contractor, and can name your price,"

Warren inserted, and Greg's eyes swung to him. "You'll be on your own in the decision making. We need to have plausible deniability if anything goes wrong."

"Of course," Greg replied, shaking his head. If anything went south, they needed a fall guy, and that would be him in this scenario. Not much different from the dark ops his teams performed under his command when he was active duty.

God, why did this stupid idea suddenly sound so intriguing? Why did he think he might be able to make it work? And why in the hell did he suddenly think it was just what he needed to break out of the funk he'd been living in for four years?

"I can get you a list of potential hires, newly retired SEALs, and the president says anything else you need," Warren continued quickly. "All we need is your commitment."

The room went silent, and Greg looked deeply into each man's eyes as he pondered a decision. What the hell did he have to lose? If he didn't agree, he'd just die a slow, agonizing death in his recliner at home. At only forty-seven and still fit, that could be a lot of years spent in that chair.

"Get me the Intel, the list, and the contract," he said, and a surge of adrenaline made his knees weak.

He was back in the game.

Chapter 1

MICHAEL HAMPTON HEARD the phone ring. Several times. He shut off the machine, turned, snagged his phone from the workbench and stepped outside. The Texas daylight was fading. He stared at the Caller ID name and froze. Why the hell would his old commander be calling him? When his commander rang through a second time, Michael hit Talk and said, "Sir? What's up?"

"I need you."

Michael winced. "I'm not in the business anymore, sir. I'm private now. I walked away, built a new life. I made it out, and I'm staying out."

"One of your old unit was murdered."

Michael froze. He didn't want to know. "Murdered?" he asked, then shook his head. It didn't matter. He was out now. "It's too late."

"It was Sammy Austen."

Michael sucked in his breath, pinching the bridge of his nose as his eyes closed in pain. Even when you had a team of alpha males, one was slightly behind the others. The one everyone else would keep a little bit more of an eye on. Capable, yes. They were all determined, strong young men. But each team had that one guy who was slightly behind the others. The one who was ever-so-slightly *less* than the others. Sammy was that one. Yet, put him among civilians, and he'd stand out as the ultimate cream of the crop. Skills were judged more harshly within the SEALs.

In a cold voice Michael asked, "What happened?"

"He was undercover, getting intel on a businessman bankrolling a terrorist cell in your corner of the world. A highly thought of businessman with aspirations to get into politics. Sammy volunteered to go in as Sammy Leacock."

"When?" His tone hard, his heart aching, Michael waited for the answers he needed, an ugly resolve setting in.

"He went in three weeks ago. His body was found yesterday morning."

"How?"

"A bullet to the back of the head. His hands and feet bound."

"Execution style." Michael's tone was clipped. Both men knew he'd seen this many times before.

"Yes. We're assuming his cover was blown, and that's not all," the commander continued. "He wasn't found alone. A young woman, a maid from the same household, was found beside him. Same thing—hands and feet tied, shot in the back of the head."

"Was she one of yours?"

"No, she was an innocent civilian."

"Do we know that for sure?" As soon as he realized he had said that *we* pronoun, he knew mentally he'd jumped back on ship. After one year away and saying no since forever in his head, at the first sign of helping a brother, he was right there. Unfortunately, he hadn't been in time to save Sammy.

"As far as we have been able to track down, she's not associated with any intel group. She had worked for over six months at the household. Her background suggests she came from a poor family, has little education and had done well for herself by becoming a maid at this place. Her wages were decent. Her bank account was healthy, although not exorbitant, but aligned with what she should be making there."

"Are you suggesting she might've gotten involved with Sammy, and both of them were taken out?"

"I can only surmise that. Sammy was always a ladies' man. If anything was going on between them, it's plausible for the group to take her out on the suspicion she might've known too much. If they wanted to make Sammy disappear, they would have taken her out anyway. Less people to ask questions."

"Was it just the two of them?"

"Yes. Both were buried in shallow graves, although *buried* is probably not quite the right word. They certainly weren't fully covered."

"Odd. Burial interrupted maybe?"

"It doesn't matter why. What matters is that we find out who did this to Sammy and that we get the intel we need on those behind the terrorist cell."

"Sammy was still active. So why isn't his team going in and finding out?" Michael shook his head. "I understand keeping this quiet, but there is off-grid, and then there is *off-grid*."

"I have permission to go completely off-grid. I can have anybody with a dissociation to Sammy."

"Then I'm not your man. Anybody who checks my background will know perfectly well that Sammy and I served together."

"I have a new identity for you, ready to go. We'll keep Michael for your first name, but you'll need to darken your hair and skin for a bit more Mexican-heritage look. It helps that you speak Spanish already if necessary."

Michael thought about that for a long moment. "Won't have to do too much to my skin. I've been outside a lot lately."

"Good. Are you in?"

Michael thought about it long and hard for all of thirty seconds. But there was really no other answer. Once a SEAL, always a SEAL, and he never left anybody behind. Sammy had gone down in the line of duty. But, if he had any chance to find out who had done this—and make sure they paid for it too—then Michael was there. In a curt voice he said, "I'm in."

MERCY ROMANO STARED at the small envelope of personal possessions gathered from her older sister's body. After the shock of identifying the body as Anna, all Mercy took away was a heavy heart and this small 6" x 9" brown envelope.

She entered her apartment, boiled water for tea, prepared her teapot and sat down heavily at her kitchen table. "Anna, what kind of trouble did you get yourself into?"

Of course, there was no answer. There was never an answer. Her sister had been a wild card. Running fast and loose in her teen years, experimenting with everything from married men to hard drugs. When she'd taken off the last time, that had been it. Mercy had never seen her sister again. Her mother had refused to talk about her as well, leaving Mercy as the only child left. The only child who was expected to be perfect, to do better than her sister had done, to be the one who succeeded. Mercy had grown up watching her sister's failed attempts to meet her mother's stringent expectations. Punished, trying again, failing, punished, and finally not even bothering to try. Instead, she'd gone in the opposite direction: completely wild.

"I hope you at least had some good years in there, girl," she said out loud as the teakettle whistled, and she steeped her tea.

Her words brought tears to her eyes. Nobody should have to bury their sister. Especially not one she'd tried so hard to find so they could reconnect. And with considerable effort. Her sister had even changed her name to Gardini to distance herself further from her family. When Mercy did find Anna, every attempt Mercy made had been completely shunned. Obviously, in her sister's mind, Mercy was in the same category as her mother and, therefore, intolerable.

Mercy had to admit it had been a pretty rough childhood for herself as well. But she had survived. She was now an adult and alone in the world. Her mother had wanted Mercy to be a doctor or a lawyer. That didn't work out so well. She never got the marks to make it. So she worked in marketing. Far enough away from mother's choice to feel Mercy had made that choice herself. But it was stressful, each new job something she had to do perfectly or her job was on the line. Maybe after this she'd change her line of work. Find something easier. Less stressful. As it were, she often came home and unwound by dancing her evening away.

Belonging to a dance troupe in Houston had been the only outlet in her life that she never let her mother interfere with. Mercy was good, but she would never be a good-enough professional dancer for her mother.

She loved the group she danced with. She loved the fact she could go out several nights a week and blast away stress from work. She could use a session right now as she looked at all she had left of her sister.

The envelope held nothing personal. Nothing to say where she had lived before or how she'd lived. Mercy had yet to see her sister's belongings. Although what belongings Anna could possibly have, Mercy didn't know. Her sister had been reported missing from her job as a live-in maid at John Freeman's residence, the up-and-coming politician, investment banker, and a local celebrity. So no furniture, no pets, probably some personal clothing other than her maid uniform, and what else? Anna was never one for hobbies or reading.

Mercy shook her head. "Did you enjoy that job? Were you happy sweeping and vacuuming, washing windows and walls? How ironic is that? One of the biggest fights between you and Mom was you refusing to do any housework, and yet, that's what you ended up doing as a career."

Oh, Mercy wished she could talk to her sister. With a cup of tea in her hand, she wondered why so much had gone so wrong in Anna's life.

Mercy presumed Anna had personal possessions, and so Mercy needed to contact Anna's boss. Mercy picked up the phone, still looking at the odd assortment of items given to her in the envelope. A necklace, a cheap ring, keys, and a couple crumpled one-dollar bills. Nothing else.

Where were the rest of her sister's things?

Mercy stared at phone and slumped in her chair. Now what? The police had been pretty noncommittal, saying they had no leads at this time, but they were working on it. If they had no leads, what the hell was she supposed to do to find out more?

She dialed Detective Robertson who had contacted her regarding her sister's death. When he answered his cell phone, she asked, "Where would the rest of Anna's personal belongings be?"

She could hear the confusion in his voice when he said, "I don't believe any were handed over to us. We searched her room at the mansion. However, it was already cleaned out. Are you looking for something in particular?"

"I won't know until I see it," she said. "I wanted to keep something as a memento of her. A sweater, a blanket, a shawl. … Something to remember her by."

"Let me get back to you."

He hung up, and she sat with her phone on the table and stared at her notepad. "None of this makes any sense." She rose and poured another hot cup of tea. By the time she sat down again, teacup in hand, her phone rang.

"I just confirmed with the estate," Detective Robertson said. "They said her belongings were handed over to us. I, however, can't find any notes about that, so I need to track down those possessions. The housekeeper also said that, if she finds anything else, they will call us." The detective's voice lowered. "Do you know a Sammy Leacock?"

She shook her head even though he couldn't see her, then

said, "No. I don't know that name, but I haven't spoken to my sister in a long time, so I have no idea what her friend group looks like now."

"Okay. If we find out anything, I'll notify you."

And she had to be satisfied with that. Or did she? She stared at the phone number she'd called first. She had three weeks of compassionate leave—only the first week was paid—which she could take to figure out what happened to her sister. Although she wasn't allowed to muddle into the police investigation, a vacancy for a maid had just opened up.

Surely she'd get answers that way.

Chapter 2

SURPRISED THAT SHE actually got the job, but understanding she'd been taken on temporarily as the housekeeper was short staffed and desperate, Mercy started in her sister's old position while her references were checked. Her fake resume and fake references. But it was hard to relax. Not only was it a new job, but she was here under a guise. Something that made her uncomfortable. She was honest and moral and this went against everything she held dear—but her sister had been murdered. And the answers were here. She knew it. And she refused to walk away because it was 'wrong.'

Then there was the unexpected emotion attached to walking in her sister's footsteps.

Expecting someone to notice the resemblance to her sister every moment although they had little familial resemblance growing up, she kept her head down and her hands busy.

Taking her sister's place at the big house was fine in theory, but the reality was a whole lot dirtier. Mercy scrubbed the floors, dusted and wiped the moldings, and was now washing and wiping the tops of window frames and doors. Even though she'd been raised by an Italian mother obsessed with cleaning, this was a whole new level. Mercy didn't know if the housekeeper was obsessed with catching every last dust mite or if this was the owner's obsession. He wasn't married, so there was no wife to blame.

It didn't matter. Mercy had done nothing but clean since she'd arrived forty-eight hours earlier. She knew she was blessed as the job gave her an opportunity to check up on her sister's last-known whereabouts, but Mercy had been so busy she'd barely had a chance to think. The housekeeper had been extremely vocal about making sure Mercy didn't dawdle.

Dawdle? Jesus, she'd never worked so hard in her life, thinking how hellish her sister's career choice had been. Yet, she had lasted here six months. Mercy was afraid she wouldn't last the week, much less three of them. And she could never get her sister to clean the room they shared when they were growing up. How had Anna appeased Martha all those months? Her sister's idea of changing the bed had been to straighten it instead of taking off the sheets.

Which reminded Mercy, she had to change out the linens in the guest bedrooms today as company was coming.

Mercy's employment here included room and board. She was sure she was sleeping in the same room as Anna had been. She hadn't had a chance to rest long enough to check it out though. Supposedly she was allowed to stay in the maid's quarters for her first three months, but staying longer was a discussion Martha would have with Mercy after her trial period ended.

That didn't sound normal.

But nothing was normal about this place. She asked about the previous maid but had gotten no reaction from anybody. She pinched her lips shut and kept going.

Another new employee had been hired the day after Mercy had arrived.

They should hire another maid, but that was unlikely at the moment. The housekeeper had mentioned in passing about big changes to come but Mercy wouldn't be here by the time those changes were put in place. So the two of them worked hard. The new guy was working as a gardener, a pool boy, and a chauffeur, plus other odd jobs. A lot of work for the new guy. Especially since the estate covered ten acres. Located outside of Houston in one of the wealthy suburbs, it was far enough away from Houston to have privacy but close enough to have access to all the amenities a big city offered.

And it was run by a fanatical housekeeper.

Mercy didn't have much time to ponder why. She had to head to the owner's office and return to cleaning. The guest coming today would be in the owner's office a lot of the time. This gave Mercy a chance to snoop in Mr. Freeman's business, because anything estate-related might be connected to her sister's murder and needed digging into. Not knowing was consuming her thoughts. She might be scared to take this step but to *not* find out more about her sister's murder and then to have regrets about that for the rest of her life … well, that would be impossible to live with.

Mercy wasn't a troublemaker by nature. In fact, she went out of her way to be nonconfrontational. It was one of the reasons she was well-liked at work—she didn't buck the system. She was a team player when she had to be, but she preferred to work independently. Often she took the lead on new projects. Then, when she had to, she'd set out the rules and expect others to follow. But here she was in the subservient role, bringing up all kinds of horrible and traumatic childhood memories. She had a new appreciation for menial labor workers though.

What if Mr. Freeman—or worse, Martha—caught Mercy snooping in his office? She had yet to meet the owner of the house, although she'd seen him in passing. So far he'd ignored her. She gathered she was not deemed worthy to speak to.

She walked into the office and stood in the middle of the double doors, studying the huge dark mahogany style office. It was somber, sober, and depressing. She walked to the curtains and opened them. She checked to see if clouds of dust rose with the movement.

But of course not. Her sister had likely cleaned them once a week. Knowing Mercy retraced every step her sister had made before her death brought up nostalgic memories that were hard to keep down. From her cleaning cart, she pulled out the spray bottle, the squeegee and the microfiber cloth to clean and dry the window and to avoid smears and then moved on to the next one.

"Aren't you done in here yet?" Martha asked from the doorway.

Mercy looked at her boss and shook her head. "No. I'm sorry. I just started in here."

With a heavy and overexaggerated sigh, Martha shook her head. "I don't know if this will work out so well. We need somebody who's efficient."

Mercy could feel her irritation rising. She stuffed it down deep. "I'm sorry. I'm trying to learn how you want the jobs done. I'll be better next time."

"If you stay here that long." Martha sniffed. "Mr. Freeman only keeps the best staff."

Holding back her tongue, Mercy meekly nodded and pointed. "If you don't mind, I'll return to cleaning windows."

Martha nodded. "You may. Let me know when you're done in this room."

As soon as Martha left, Mercy turned her attention to the other windows and cleaned her way through them. They had to be cleaned from the outside as well. Even from Mr. Freeman's office, Mercy could see cobwebs were collecting under and around the exterior shutters.

She glanced at his desk and wondered if she dared open a drawer. For all she knew, everything here was wired to an alarm. Although that thought did take her paranoia to a whole new level. Still, how would she find out anything about her sister otherwise? And it seemed she only cleaned this room weekly.

She couldn't be here for more than the three weeks she'd booked off from work, but it already looked like it would be a very long, hard three weeks. She wondered at her foolishness. But, at the same time, her sister had died because of this place. Mercy wanted to know who the hell was responsible. From Detective Robertson, she understood Sammy had been the previous gardener-chauffeur guy and had been killed at her side. Maybe they had hooked up. She didn't know, but she wanted to. She didn't have a clue how to find out.

Taking a chance, she took a duster to the desk, expecting somebody to jump in and scream at her any second now. She assumed there were cameras in every room, she just couldn't see them.

She quickly went about dusting the desk surface, pulling the handles on the drawers, opening them ever-so-slightly to get the layer of dust on the top edge, closing them quickly and moving to the next one. Thereafter, she walked to the large oak filing cabinets, repeating the process. All of the cabinet doors were locked. When finally done, she headed toward the door, only to see the owner standing there, his hands in his pockets studying her, a cold look in his eyes. She froze, then gave him a bright smile and said, "Good morning."

There was something almost reptilian about that gaze. Then again she was looking for reasons to not like him. He'd done nothing for her sister. He had treated her as a slave. The man inclined his head gently and stepped out of the way as she rushed past him. She quickly took her cleaning cart farther down the hall to the first of the guest bedrooms.

She could feel Mr. Freeman's eyes boring into her back. But she dared not look behind her. She had to appear completely unconcerned, but the timing was suspicious. Did it have anything to do with her working around the desk? Did he have cameras in there or sensors that went off? If he was into anything corrupt or illegal, it would make sense that he did have high security measures in place. And then again maybe he had come to his office to work.

She put the thought out of her head for the rest of the day. When it was her lunch break, she went to the kitchen, where the cook had set out a sandwich and a glass of water for her.

In a low voice she asked, "Is there any place outside I can sit?"

The cook pointed to a small veranda off to the left. "Staff goes there. Do not go around to any of the other verandas." His tone was hard, but more because he was busy. Not because he was unfriendly. She hoped …

Taking her water and plate, she went outside, sat in the shade and ate. This was a world so vastly removed from her own. She couldn't imagine her sister living here.

Anna was not the same sister Mercy used to know. What the hell had happened? It wasn't that cleaning wasn't a good job. But Mercy had never seen her sister work at anything.

She was almost done with the sandwich when she looked up to see the gardener walking past with great big clippers in his hand and a handful of weeds as he studied the bed to the side of the veranda. Something about his profile caught her attention.

He had a weathered look to his face, like someone who was outdoors a lot. That certainly fit his role. But the way he studied the bed, as if his senses were on alert, was strange. She finished her last bite of food, grabbed her glass and had a long sip. Swallowed. "Good afternoon, I'm Mercy Romano."

He lifted his head and looked at her. Piercing blue eyes pinned her in place. It was almost like he had a computerized brain, cataloguing who she was, what she was, where she was, and why she was here.

When he turned his gaze to look at the door behind her, it was as if he had released her from some invisible thread.

He inclined his head and said in a low voice, deep and soft, "Good afternoon."

His voice was so at odds to what she expected that she was startled for a moment. "I just arrived here myself," she said. "We started a day apart."

His gaze softened ever-so-slightly. He nodded. "Congratulations on the job."

"You too."

He bent down and pulled up a minuscule weed that had dared to pop up through the layer of heavy rocks, then walked away.

Mercy stood and stared at the gardener. There was something about him, like he was ready to pounce at a moment's notice. His movements were controlled and yet casual. She couldn't quite explain it, but something was so very powerful about his physique. She wondered how it could be so opposite to what she had imagined a gardener would be like. For some reason she thought the gardener would be lanky, relaxed, easygoing—nothing like him at all.

He hadn't told her what his name was either. Still with time left on her break, she picked up her plate to return inside. Once in the kitchen and under the eagle eyes of the chef, she winced as she loaded her dishes into the dishwasher.

With an apologetic smile she asked, "Is there any coffee?"

At that his face broke into a smile, and he pointed to a coffeepot on the side. "Help yourself. Cream's in the fridge."

"Black is fine for me. Thanks." She poured her coffee and, with a small nod, she said again, "Thank you." And she walked back out onto the veranda.

She'd return to work early but not too early. It was pretty damn hard to look at the walls she'd be scrubbing next and find any kind of enjoyment in the task. She understood lots of woman found satisfaction in cleaning houses, but there was clean, and then there was being stupid. This wasn't a hospital. It didn't need to be scrubbed down the same way, but that was what she felt she was doing. Then again, maybe this was a normal seasonal cleaning event. Or were they erasing signs of somebody having been here, like her sister?

MICHAEL HEADED TO the garden shed where he replaced the shears. Normally yard work was something he enjoyed. But nothing was enjoyable about this job. Something was seriously wrong on this estate. Sammy must've known. How could he possibly have let his guard down long enough to be caught up in a web that took his life? Michael also didn't understand the relationship he had with the woman killed alongside him.

The new maid appeared shy, quiet. Then that was probably the right personality for the position. Whereas, he had to work at being deferential. But years in the military helped. Having completed his circle of the large yard, he headed to the huge Lincoln he was supposed to drive the owner around in. It needed a good wash and a vacuum. He set about moving it to where the drains were and brought up the hoses and the sponges. Even though it was lunchtime, and he had yet to eat, he started scrubbing the vehicle on the inside. This gave him an excellent opportunity to examine the vehicle completely. He hoped to find something in the seats or pockets.

By the time he was done, he had found a few pieces of change that had fallen from various pockets, a couple receipts—one for gas and another for something from a local lingerie shop—which he tucked away for further scrutinizing, and a little bit of garbage that wasn't helpful. When he had the inside of the vehicle vacuumed and wiped down, he turned his attention to the front seat. There he carefully went through the glove box, wiping inside and outside, checking for anything suspicious as he went.

He was hoping Sammy might have left a message of some kind to say what the hell had gone wrong. This was Michael's second day. He'd moved into the servants' quarters but had spent the initial part of his first day getting his marching orders from both Bruce, his direct boss, and Martha, the head housekeeper. Afterward, Michael spent the bulk of his day in the gardens, acclimating himself to the layout here while performing his gardener's duties. Also looking for ground level access to the two lower floors of the mansion that Ice had been able to verify via blueprints and subsequent building licenses for add-ons. He hadn't found any yet, but he wouldn't stop looking. So Michael hadn't had a chance to check out Sammy's rooms too intently. But they were pristine and empty.

Apparently, there had been a high turnover of staff here. Was it possible that Sammy's belongings might still be here? Michael hoped they hadn't been packed up and disposed of yet. It could be on his list of jobs to do, in which case he had no intention of dumping it off just anywhere but going through it all. Still, that job hadn't been given to him.

He finished detailing the inside of the car, turned on the water and worked on the outside of the vehicle.

The Lincoln was brand-new. It was in great shape, and not a speck of dirt was found after a careful check. Michael was sure no fingerprints were inside. But he also couldn't find any fingerprints in the back, the passenger section. So somebody had recently wiped down the vehicle. Why?

He still had to do the trunk, but the key was jammed in the lock, making him all the more interested in getting inside it. He quickly finished shampooing the vehicle and rinsed it down again. With a light wax he gave it a good shiny coat. Then he popped the trunk with a screwdriver. After a few minutes of playing with the mechanism, he extracted the broken-off key and got the lock to work again. He turned his attention to the empty trunk.

He took his time fixing the carpet—that looked like it had been pulled out at the back—as he carefully checked under it for any bloodstains. He could only use his experienced eye. To do anything else would raise suspicions from the many security guards about the property. Someone would notice. Hell, it felt like he was watched as soon as he'd arrived. The back of the trunk was cleaned out, and he couldn't find anything here other than a few scratches but after closer examination they weren't made by fingernails as he'd feared. More from suitcases or boxes having been loaded and unloaded by someone who hadn't been as careful as they could have been.

If any DNA was on the inside or within those scratches, they needed to know. Forensic evidence went a long way to making a conviction. On the other hand, how he would get that evidence so it would be admissible in court was a completely different story.

That wasn't his problem—that was the prosecutor's. Michael's problem was to find out who the hell had taken Sammy's life. If that asshole was still alive by the end of this special op, Michael would be very surprised.

A shadow came from the corner of the house. He shut the lid, turned to see the housekeeper, accompanied by one of the men who worked in the house who had brought down several boxes. Michael walked over to get the housekeeper's instructions.

"Take all this to the police, please. You're expected to pick up Mr. Freeman here at four. You've enough time to drop them off and return."

Michael nodded, grabbed the keys, walked over to the Lincoln and backed it up. There he popped the trunk again, having no trouble with it now, and quickly loaded the boxes. He knew already about the tracker on the Lincoln, so he was limited as to how far he could travel without being questioned about any detours. As soon as he pulled out of the driveway, he picked up his phone. Rather than making a call that might be overheard, he sent a text.

He didn't know if the boxes contained Anna or Sammy's stuff or something completely different, but Michael wouldn't have much time or opportunity to check it out. What he needed was somebody to meet him at the police station and take possession of the material.

At the station, he pulled into the back of the building. He hopped out and froze at the sight of two people he hadn't expected to see here.

One man stepped out from the open doorway of the building. The man waiting off to the side joined him.

Michael nodded his head at Merk and Levi and took several steps off to the side as he punched the button on his key to open the trunk. He knew them by sight, by name and by profession. They had gone private after leaving the military, stepping out of all of it. The fact that the commander had brought them in too was very interesting. He must really need to keep this low-key.

The two men pulled out the boxes from the back of the

vehicle and opened the flaps on one.

Michael pointed to a small paperweight, saying, in a low and hard voice, "I recognize that. It's Sammy's."

In a louder voice Levi said, "Thanks for bringing this by." With a curt nod, he slipped Michael a small piece of paper, grabbed a box and walked into the station.

Michael placed the rest of the boxes on the ground, knowing he'd get any details about their contents later. Now that he'd confirmed at least some of the possessions were Sammy's, Michael could only hope there'd be something helpful to this op, but he doubted it. It wouldn't be Sammy's way. Any information would be well hidden. And that meant in his own apartment. He'd searched it several times, but he'd look again.

Time was running out for him to pick up Mr. Freeman by four o'clock. Michael got back into the vehicle and started the engine. He drove to the parking lot exit and sat there for a moment, letting the traffic pass. When there was an opening, he pulled out.

He thought about all the avenues one could take when one left the military and about all the damn good men he had met over the years. Levi and Merk were two of them.

At the next light, Michael opened the folded note Levi had passed on and read the message. "Good to see you back. Come to work for us when this is over."

Michael shook his head. *I'm not ready for that, Levi.*

He drove back the way he'd come to the estate. He'd only re-entered this world because of Sammy.

It wasn't what he wanted to do again.

And the nightmares ... Sometimes the nightmares were crippling. Unless Levi could give Michael a lifestyle that allowed him to move forward with a personal life and still help others while keeping the nightmares to a minimum, then Michael wasn't interested. On the other hand, it was pretty hard not to see how the adrenaline coursing through his system was what he loved, how much he enjoyed being in the field, how much this lifestyle suited him. He was good at what he did. He was just burned out.

Besides, this wasn't the time to make decisions about his future. Everything was certainly on hold until he got justice for Sammy.

Chapter 3

TWO DAYS LATER, Mercy had a lot more respect for her sister and others working in this career and a whole lot less respect for the employers who they worked for. Such a cold atmosphere surrounded Mercy that she didn't understand how her sister had handled it. It took a couple days for Mercy to get accustomed to the physical work and to the sheer drudgery of it. Without mental stimulation, it was more difficult for her. She loved a challenge, but dusting faster wasn't one she could get behind. Still, she was no slouch and could do the work, but she was grateful she was only here temporarily.

Added to that was the frustration of being here for several days now and not finding anything of interest. How was she supposed to learn anything about her sister's murder when all she did was dust and clean and scrub?

She'd gone over her own bedroom top to bottom but hadn't found anything saying her sister had ever been there. Surely someone here at the mansion knew something. Yet no one talked to her.

Mercy hadn't had a chance to contact the detective again either. So much tension was in this house that it made her look around every corner as if she were watched. Yet she never saw anyone. But the feeling remained.

She was very mindful of the fact cameras were likely everywhere, giving her limited places to search unobserved. She tried to be friendlier to the staff, but that was like butting up against a wall of ice. Knowing her behavior was monitored, her actions watched and her words analyzed, she stuck to herself more and more. She ate alone; she worked mostly alone and had very little social contact with the outside world. If this was her sister's life, she pitied her.

Surely there was a boyfriend, someone who cared. As far as anyone here knew, Mercy Romano was not related to Anna Gardini—she hoped. Therefore, Mercy had no right to ask questions outside of morbid curiosity into a dead person's life. And that was likely to draw attention to her. More attention she didn't want. It seemed like everyone knew she was failing to live up to the housekeeper's expectations as it were. Maybe it was nerves, but it seemed like people were watching her.

Several times she'd spun around sure that she was being watched—only to find no one was there.

She walked into the kitchen storage area and put away the dusting rags and other materials. It was time to work on the windows in the dining room. She grabbed the cleaning supplies she needed, the small ladder and headed to the dining room. And stopped. It wasn't empty. In a low tone she said, "I'm scheduled to clean windows in here. Will that bother you?"

Mr. Freeman, the owner, looked up, a harried look in his eyes as he glanced from her to the windows and back again. "No, that's fine. Go ahead."

She hurried to the first of the three huge windows to set

out her short ladder and climbed up. As she cleaned, she glanced around, noting the cameras on the far side. Of course. She couldn't look for anything in this room, even without him here.

She was working on the second window when one of his associates walked in and said, "We're having trouble with the security cameras inside the house."

"What kind of trouble?"

"They keep flickering off and on."

"Well then, call the damn security company."

"I have. They're sending a man out."

"Is it affecting the outside security?" This time Mr. Freeman's voice was harder.

His associate nodded. "Yes, sir."

Mercy turned her gaze away after catching the conversation. She didn't want to remind them she was here. But a problem with the security system could be a great thing to help her snoop around some. However, the main outage seemed to be on the grounds of the estate. So the "flickering off and on" inside the mansion didn't really give her a precise window of opportunity. Her chances of successfully using this interruption in security were obviously extremely small.

"Double the perimeter security," Mr. Freeman said.

"Already done."

Mr. Freeman nodded. "The individuals in the security room must watch all the time, in case the new man is outside. Make sure he's sticking to his job and not to my business."

The associate said, "That I can do." He turned on his heels and walked out.

Mercy finished the second window and moved her ladder

to the third one. There she climbed to the top of the ladder and scrubbed down the window.

"How are you finding your new job?"

His tone of voice and words directed at her startled her enough she almost lost her footing. She grabbed hold of the ladder. When balanced again, she looked at Mr. Freeman and said with a small smile, "It's fine."

His gaze was piercing as he studied her face. She swallowed hard and dropped her gaze, hopefully appropriately subservient. When she glanced back up his head was already down, looking at the papers on the big dining room table. He had a huge desk in his office, and she wasn't sure why he was here, but binders and documents were all up and down one side of the long table.

She finished the window, folded her ladder, grabbed her cleaning supplies and walked past him. And she paused. "I don't know if you have an assistant or not, but I do have a little experience helping my mother with paperwork ... She had a small sewing business." To her horror the lie rolled off her lips naturally.

He looked up in surprise.

She gave a small smile and kept walking. She'd thrown out the bone. Whether he did anything with it or not was up to him. Back in the kitchen storage closet, she put away the cleaning supplies and looked at the schedule the housekeeper had set out for her. Mercy was scheduled for laundry. *Awesome.* She was behind. She shook her head. What's new? In the back of her mind, she wondered if Martha was intentionally setting up Mercy to fail so she would be fired.

This job left her feeling inadequate, and yet it was just

damn cleaning. With her shoulders already slumping at the thought of the ten loads still to be washed, dried, folded, and put away. She walked into the large laundry room to find a couple loads already started and several piles ready to be sorted and more to be folded. There was even ironing. Who ironed in this day and age?

These people had more money than God. Surely they could afford to buy no-iron shirts. But bellyaching never got her anywhere. She buckled down and folded the towels. She'd already had a lecture on the proper way to fold them and how everything was to be placed correctly in the cabinets. She had to admit they looked nice, but they sure weren't worth the extra work when she had so much else to do today.

This was only her second time in the laundry room on laundry duty, so she struggled to get through the instructions in her head. She looked around to see if instructions were posted on the wall in here. A piece of paper had been dropped by the door, so she walked over with a towel in her hand to pick it up, but it wasn't what she was looking for. She frowned, glanced around again and then shrugged. Minutes later the door opened, and the housekeeper walked in. "What are we looking for?"

Mercy raised her eyebrows. "Sorry?"

"Security called to let me know you were looking for something in the laundry room," she said coolly. "What were you looking for?"

Wow. I didn't realize I was under such tight observation. "The written list of instructions you verbally told me as to the exact amounts of detergent for each different load. I had hoped *that*"—she pointed to the sheet of paper on the floor—

"was the instruction sheet."

The housekeeper gave her a penetrating look and said, "I'll write them down and bring it in." She walked from the room, closing the door firmly behind her.

The trouble was that *snick* of the door closing was almost like a prison door snapping shut. *Unbelievable.* She would be here for several hours no matter how much was on her schedule. No way she could get through these massive amounts of towels and bedding and get the ironing done.

With a sinking feeling, she realized it was time to buckle down and get it done. She quickly realized how futile was her hope to find out more about Anna while serving as a maid here. Mercy needed to get the hell away and go home. There was no other option. Maybe that was what this was all about. Maybe she had to get to the point where she accepted she would have to leave this up to the police.

Two hours later she was still working in the laundry room when the housekeeper returned. She carried a sheet of paper and put it on the wall beside the machines. "Here are the instructions." She walked out without saying another word.

Mercy glanced at her watch. It was almost noon, and she was well past her time allotted to be done with the laundry. Yet, she was only halfway done. She knew at the end of her shift she would get another lecture, if not get fired. She shook her head. Maybe that would be for the best. She was well known to be a hardworking staff member at her real job, but here she had a sense of never doing enough, never being appreciated for what she had done. However, her fighting spirit and her sense of pride remained intact.

It took her another hour plus to get through the rest of

the laundry. When she walked into the kitchen looking for some lunch, she found a premade sandwich sitting on the counter, the edges already dry. She glanced at the chef.

He said, his voice full of irritation, "You're late."

She nodded warily. "Three and half hours in the laundry room." She snatched her sandwich and a glass of milk and went outside. She sat down, looking at the immaculate gardens, thinking about security cameras flickering, realizing even with those minuscule and unknown windows of opportunity, there was still no chance for her to find out anything without getting caught. Surely it was time to leave this foolhardy mission. But, if she did, she felt she would be giving up on her sister.

BACK AT THE estate Michael changed his plans when he saw repairmen working on the security cameras. He'd done a good job sabotaging the system without making it look like it had been sabotaged. He'd have to do his best to screw up any attempt to fix it. Or at least make this a long-drawn-out process so he could get a secure window of time to search the estate. As it was, he struggled to maintain the whole "Yes, master" syndrome, the obedience here that was demanded.

While in the military he had no problem obeying orders as he'd believed in the system. Now he wanted to punch some heads to get the information he needed. One of these bastards had likely murdered Sammy. Michael wanted to know who. This morning not once did security figure out that Michael had made several tiny slices in the wires, then flooded them with the sprinklers. They were completely drenched and flickering. The security system would short out from the water.

He'd broken the line on a more remote section of the gardens as well to confuse those trying to fix the system. He needed to delay them in repairing the security cameras. The inside security system was a little bit more complicated. He only had access to a small portion of it but had done what he could with what he had.

He was no electrician, but he was pretty damn handy with wire cutters. At the end of the day, the security system was still not resolved, and he headed back to his small apartment over the older garage used mostly for storage and when doing vehicle maintenance. That's when he caught sight of the new maid again. He watched her. He'd passed her several times as she sat on the small porch, eating what looked like dry bread. He didn't think she'd last long.

She looked tired, worn out and, like him, frustrated. He had to wonder at that. Back in his apartment he made himself a sandwich. He hadn't picked up much in the way of groceries but didn't want to eat at the big house, particularly after seeing the food served to the new maid, Mercy. Thankfully it was a choice for him.

Then he got into his own vehicle and headed into town. There he picked up a few more groceries and stopped in at the coffee shop. With his laptop and secure Wi-Fi, he checked in for any information from the detective. A message from Ice waited for him. He smiled. Ice was an old friend. He knew her better than he knew Levi. But then, Ice had flown Michael's ass out of trouble more than a couple times.

Michael owed her his life.

She sent him her complete intel files she'd created on Sammy and everyone else in the house. The detective had sent Michael what the commander had already sent, except some files were more extensive. Michael read through them but found nothing new other than the proof of a relationship between Sammy and Anna, the maid.

Obviously the killer decided that, if one was culpable of spying, likely the other was involved as well. So Anna could've been an innocent bystander, but, by association, she'd been taken out.

He opened the folder he'd received from the commander on Anna Gardini and froze. Because there in front of him was an image of the woman who looked so similar to Mercy. He quickly searched the family history, found Anna's name change. Romano was her family name. Further research quickly revealed a sister. *Mercy.* "How the hell did Freeman's security not catch this? Or are they fully aware and will just kill her when deemed necessary?"

He settled back and sipped his coffee as he wondered, "What the hell are you doing here, you fool?" He shook his head disturbed.

Was she here by choice? He couldn't come up with one damn good reason why she had been coerced here … Or was she really out of work and had asked to take her sister's place?

As he thought about the reasons why he was here, it was a little hard to ignore the fact that maybe, just maybe, she wanted answers too.

But the last thing he needed was a nosy amateur sleuth asking questions around the place, mucking up his undercover investigation, distracting him from his op. And he didn't give a damn how sexy she was.

Chapter 4

A T THE END of her shift, Mercy grabbed a light sweater and left to go for a walk. She had a decision to make. She'd just received the harshest reprimand of her adult life. Still smarting, she headed down the driveway to the gates.

There was no reason why she shouldn't be allowed to leave. She wasn't a prisoner. With the outside security all messed up as it was, the gates were still open. With her shoulders hunched, and her head tucked down against the blowing wind, she walked down the driveway. She stood in front of the security camera so they could see her for a moment, and then she walked through the open gateway. Out on the main road, she chose one shoulder and kept walking.

It was hard to imagine being as useless as the housekeeper made Mercy feel. The fact that she couldn't find any information about her sister just compounded the problem. Everywhere she went, she imagined her sister's hands doing the same work she was doing. Her fingers stroking along the same walls, the same windows.

There was such a sense of connectedness to Anna in the mansion that, for the first time in a long time, Mercy realized how much she had missed her sister's presence over the years. Had her sister missed her? Or had she written off her mother and sister and not given them a thought? Mercy would like to think her sister had regretted some of her actions. But it was hard to say.

She wasn't more than a block away when a light rain fell. "Great. Just what I need right now." She was sore and tired and almost ready to call a cab and to keep on going. But she had her meager belongings in her room which she would prefer not to leave behind. Neither could she afford to walk away from her car. She didn't want anyone from the Freeman estate tracking her down and finding her. She hadn't even brought her purse with her. So she had to return.

The light rain became a soaking drizzle. Even knowing it was foolish to keep going, she couldn't stop. She was desperate to get as many feet between her and the nasty job she'd left behind—at least for a moment. Finally her footsteps slowed, and she turned reluctantly to retrace her steps.

She hadn't been walking toward the house for more than a few seconds when a truck slowed. She froze as it pulled up beside her. Behind the steering wheel was the gardener. She frowned as the power window dropped so he could talk to her.

"Do you want a ride back?"

She shook her head instinctively.

He gave a disgusted snort. "Yes, you do. You're soaked to the skin. If you want to keep your job, you can't afford to get sick."

For a brief moment she thought about that being a lovely way to get out of her job. Obviously they wouldn't keep her if she was sick. Not these people. A person who worked for them was just a number, and more numbers were easily found. She put a hand on the door handle and opened it, then hesitated.

He shook his head and said, "I'm not worried about the seats getting wet. Hop in, and let's get you back to dry off."

Without making a comment, she scrambled into the front seat and closed the door. Reaching for the seat belt, she buckled in. He pulled back onto the pavement of the deserted road.

"What are you doing out here anyway?"

"Getting some fresh air and leaving the oppression behind," she said quietly.

He shot her a curious glance. "Is it that bad?"

She nodded. "Yes, it is."

"Time for a new job?"

She stared at the gray skies, the rain now running heavily down the window, and muttered, "I don't know."

"Why did you take your sister's place?"

She gasped. "What are you talking about?"

The look in his eyes made her realize he was no fool. She didn't know what his role in this business was, but it was obvious he wouldn't take any excuses.

She stared at her fingers for a long moment, then said, "My sister was murdered. I was hoping I could find out something about her last days. They don't even have her belongings anymore."

"Besides the utmost stupidity of your actions, did you ask the police for her belongings?"

She nodded and explained, "The detective said they hadn't received anything of hers, but they did have Sammy's belongings delivered by the estate. The detective did say he'd contact me if they found out anything new, but I haven't heard from him yet."

On that thought, she pulled out her phone from her pocket and checked for messages, but again there were none. But then, who else would contact her? Her mother was gone, now her sister too. Mercy only wanted to hear from the detective. Of course she wasn't even on his priority list.

"And, if your sister was murdered, what makes you think you'd find any information here?"

"It's where she lived, where she worked. And maybe where she had a boyfriend, but I don't know about that yet." She looked at him. "You're replacing a man who was murdered too."

He nodded. "I know. But I didn't have anything to do with either of the murders."

"Neither did I."

They came up to the gates of the estate, which were still open. He drove through and around to the back entrance to let her out. "Make sure you watch your back."

She had the door open when she understood the gist of his words. She turned back to him. "Meaning?"

"Meaning, with two dead, a third won't make any difference."

With his cryptic words ringing in her ears, she hopped out and slammed the truck door. She didn't know who he was, but he certainly didn't appear to fit the role of whatever he'd taken on here. Unless he was also a bodyguard. With eyes that looked like steel and his hard body, he had a panther's grace and the air of a predator. One that *seemed* to be in a relaxed state, looking normal, but was always ready for action, with muscles that would bunch and move on demand like the big untamed cat he was inside.

She hurried back into the house and upstairs to her small room. She passed no one on her way, but she had no illusions about being watched. She was always being watched. She'd just never caught them at it.

Once inside her room, she quickly stripped off her clothes and hopped into a hot shower. When she was warm and her hair shampooed, she stepped out and wrapped up in a big towel.

The medicine cabinet in front of her opened easily, and she took out her toothbrush. It was early yet, but she might as well get ready for bed. She needed the extra rest. While she was brushing her teeth, her eyes surveyed the cabinet. It was loose in the wall. She jiggled the corner to see if it would fall. It was only a foot and a half across, but she wasn't sure how heavy it was, although it appeared to be made of plastic.

She carefully pulled it forward and set it down on top of the sink counter. A small notebook was left in the recessed area. With excitement coursing through her, she picked up the notebook and placed it atop her clean nightie, then carefully replaced the medicine cabinet. She finished brushing her teeth and found herself looking around the small bathroom, searching for cameras.

There was always a chance this room was bugged or under video monitor, and she had to be careful. Though it was illegal, she didn't think anybody here would give a shit about laws.

She went through the motions as if going to bed—grabbed a book she had on her nightstand, crawled into bed, turned on the lamp. With the notebook tucked inside the book's pages, she opened both the book and notebook and started to read.

On the first page was her sister's name—Anna. Not knowing why her sister would have this book and why she had hidden it, Mercy flipped through the pages, finding detailed entries of things going on in the house. Curious, yet disturbed at the same time, she read her sister's notes about weapons being unloaded in the garage.

Not a gun or two but crates of them. Her heart pounding, she flipped through the pages to find more entries of random unnamed guests but no further mention of guns was made.

When she finally made her way to the end of the book, she found little personal notes about her sister being desperate to leave. She'd hooked up with Sammy, and together they planned on moving. Not around the corner where they would still be close to the mansion and could keep working here, but they would head north to get away. Anna confessed she was in love with Sammy, but something about him worried her.

Secretive, dangerous. And then she wrote the word *Trustworthy?*

Her last entry was *I have to take this chance. I can't stay where I am. I have to trust Sammy. I love him. I hope I'm doing the right thing.*

With her heart pounding and tears in her eyes, Mercy slowly lowered the book and tucked it inside her pillowcase under her head. Hearing the words in her sister's heart was so damn difficult. Mercy's own heart filled with regret about all that could have been. This notebook wouldn't convict anyone, but it could help. Except ... with all the eyes on her, how would she get it to the detective?

ICE'S INTEL CONFIRMED that Mercy had used her real name when applying for this maid position. Michael should've asked her if her employer knew who she was. It could determine if she was here on the sly or if they were aware of her connection to their previous maid. They might not have cared. On the other hand, they might care in a big way if they hadn't found out beforehand.

In his days here, he hadn't found proof of any wrongdoing. Sammy had been a good SEAL. He should've left some warning signs somewhere. It was up to Michael to find them. But he couldn't afford to take time to find something that may not exist.

He drove around to his little apartment and parked in the back. Pulling out the bag of groceries along with his laptop, he headed inside. There, he found the main door still locked to his room. The hair he had placed was still there too. He walked inside, locked the door behind him and placed his items on the counter. He checked to see if the other security measures he had put in place were untouched, and the slivers of invisible tape were still affixed randomly to all the windows—which meant nobody had entered the apartment since he'd left. At least through that door. He did a quick search of his apartment as he did every time he entered. He couldn't afford to be sloppy.

Reassured, he made himself a small pot of coffee and booted up his laptop again. He had security measures on his internet connection too that would stop others from hacking in. He'd sabotaged the security system in and around the estate but hadn't had a chance to deal with Freeman's internet feed, and he would love to get access to that. So far, he hadn't been granted entrance into the mansion long enough to even have a cup of coffee.

Now that he knew the name of the previous maid, he did a search to check out more about who Anna Romano Gardini was, what she was, and what she was doing here. The information was fairly limited, and, outside of a few mentions of her name that could be found by anybody on Google, he couldn't unearth much.

Anna had a clean driving record, no criminal record, and appeared to be in the best of health, with one issue over a decade earlier of note but not connected with gun-running terrorists. There was no explanation for why she had been here at this estate. Worst-case scenario was Anna was involved with the terrorist cell. Best-case scenario was she had gotten pulled in by Sammy and killed because she'd been in the wrong place at the wrong time. Michael hoped, for the family's sake, the latter was the case.

It was always hard for family members to understand and accept the murder of a loved one, but it was always way worse when they found out the loved one had been involved in something so terrible.

As he sat with his coffee, a text came through from Levi. One single word.

Nothing.

Michael tossed his phone on the table and walked to the small couch to sit down. *Nothing. So there's nothing in all of Sammy's belongings to indicate what the hell's going on here.* He shook his head. *Come on, Sammy. You knew better than not to leave something behind.*

He glanced out the window and saw the light going out in the new maid's room. It was awfully early for her to go to bed. On the other hand, she might've been chilled from her walk in the rain. Not to mention tired. She didn't look to be having an easy time of it in the house.

The memories triggered by being here had to be difficult. Hell, they were difficult for him, and Sammy wasn't family. He was a team member, and that made him family, but, at the moment, Michael couldn't think of Sammy as such. Michael had to stay detached.

He studied the dark side of the house now—the servants' quarters wing, as Ice's blueprint of the estate had revealed multiple tiny en suite bedrooms. Then a light at the bottom of the stairs turned on. He watched a shadow walk upstairs toward the maid's room.

The security men had rooms on the far side of the building. The maids had housing on this side. At the moment there was only one on staff. Which was ludicrous for a house this size.

He frowned and shifted slightly for a better view. He didn't know who else lived on the second floor, but no more lights were on, and only one window was on that side. He'd yet to see anyone other than the new maid use that entrance either. Thankfully she had the bedroom with the only window he could see. He waited and watched.

Suddenly the light turned on again in the maid's room. He could see the woman wave at him. The stranger left, his shadow disappearing down the stairs. He glanced back at the woman, to watch as she turned on the light. Why would somebody come to the servants' quarters at night? And why especially to her room?

"Dammit," he muttered under his breath. Her getting mixed up in this would mess with his timetable. On these undercover ops, especially when slipping in so soon after the incident, it was best to take it slow, not draw unneeded attention, let things meander along as the bad guys lose interest in the new guys.

Now he had to work faster. It would put him in more danger, but it may take some attention off the new maid.

Chapter 5

MERCY WAITED IN bed, the covers pulled up tight to her chin. Up until now, nobody had come up the stairs or passed her room over the five evenings she'd been here. Definitely nobody had come up and stopped. She could hear her heart pounding with every footstep she heard coming toward her door. She strained to hear if the person had moved on. Unfortunately it sounded like he—or she—still stood there. Why?

She cast her mind in a wide circle, figuring out why somebody would stand outside her door at night. She had engaged the inside lock, but it wasn't a high-security thing. She imagined any number of people would know how to get in without too much trouble. She slipped out from under the covers and tiptoed toward the door. She heard nothing but was not breathing any easier. Then she moved quietly over to the window. Was there a secondary exit to leave her room to get away from someone? The fact that she couldn't hear his movements made her more scared.

Surely he couldn't have crept down the stairs without her hearing.

Her sole window was nice to have but was shut due to Houston's hot muggy days and evenings. She looked out her second-floor view. There was no veranda, no fire escape or anything that would help her get down. As she looked down, she saw the grounds sloping away from the building, meaning this portion of the mansion sat on a hill, so her window was much higher than two stories.

She stared across the yard at the garage and saw a silhouette staring right back at her. She froze. It was the gardener. She pulled her robe tighter around her neck. Somebody stood at her door *and* somebody watched her from across the lawn? Neither was good. She glanced toward the door. The creaks she heard told her that whoever had come up the stairs was slowly making his way back down.

She sagged against the window edge in relief. Quickly she turned on her light. It took a little bit of the shadows away but still left her with a creepy distaste crawling all over her skin. There was no good reason for anyone to have come up the stairs to her door.

As she glanced back at the garage apartment, she wondered why the gardener remained at his window, still staring at her. He hadn't waved; he hadn't done anything but stare. Talk about unnerving. Finally she gave him a half wave, stepped away from the window, keeping a slight view of him, but just enough that he couldn't see her and turned out the light.

After a moment he stepped away. Lying down in bed, she realized for the first time what a dangerous situation she'd put herself in. She curled up in a ball and shuddered. Her sister had been murdered, for God's sake, yet Mercy had come and put herself in her sister's shoes. Up until tonight, it all had been fine. She hadn't had a second thought about her personal safety. But that fact had been brought home to her very clearly a few moments ago.

The night was long. She tossed and turned and woke up a half-dozen times, listening for sounds of somebody outside. There never was. But that didn't stop her from straining to hear. Twice she got up to look out the window but didn't see the gardener again that night.

Something was so different about him. How did he fit into this place? She could see him in the military or flying helicopters or doing something edgy as a career. Being a gardener ... not so much. As it was, he was the image she carried through her twisted dreams, some gallant knight through her fantasies.

By morning she looked the way she felt. Haggard, bags under her eyes, and tired.

She was due a couple days off but wasn't sure she'd get them, considering more company was coming. What more could be done in terms of cleaning, she didn't know. Everything had been scrubbed from top to bottom.

She made her way down to breakfast, once again having two pieces of toast and a cup of coffee while the kitchen staff remained busy. She stepped outside to eat. Immediately, she felt the muggy heat, and she contemplated her options.

Physically she'd get through another hard day of cleaning, no doubt about that. But every day was wearing her down a little more. If she didn't get her days off, she knew she couldn't maintain the exacting standards and speed the housekeeper expected. If Mercy didn't get fired, it would be suggested she quit on her own. Inasmuch as she liked that idea right now, the creep outside her door last night reminded her all too much of what her sister must've gone through. Surely something here would help Mercy find Anna's killer.

Breakfast over, Mercy walked across the front hall toward the laundry room when the house phone rang. As part of her duties, she picked it up and answered it in a formal tone, announcing the Freeman residence.

"This is Detective Sanders. I'm trying to locate the personal belongings of Anna Gardini. We have the belongings of Sammy Leacock, but those of the maid haven't arrived. We'd like to send somebody out today to pick them up."

"I'm not exactly sure where they are." She glanced up to see the housekeeper striding toward her. "Here's Martha. She's the housekeeper. She will know." Mercy held up the phone and said, "It's a detective, looking for the former maid's belongings."

The housekeeper gave him a frown as if he could possibly see it through the phone. By the looks of it, she would give it a darn good try. "Everything was handed over to the police. I already told you that," she said in a testy voice.

"I suggest you take another look, or we'll come search ourselves. *Today.*" The detective's voice came through the phone clearly. "This is a murder investigation, and we need *all* the woman's personal belongings. You are obstructing an official police investigation. Not to mention the fact the family has the right for closure. We will get a warrant if need be."

The housekeeper gave another frown but grabbed the landline phone and took it with her a short distance down the hall. "I'll see if they've been accidentally left behind." She opened a large storage closet in the front hallway. "I don't believe they're here, but I will look again."

Mercy couldn't hear the rest of the conversation. But, if the detective had said the belongings hadn't showed up at the police station, maybe, with the recent change of staff, Anna's personal things were still around. Mercy knew this detective's name was Sanders, and it was not the same one she'd been dealing with. It gave her hope to think two people were still working on this case. She carried on through to the laundry room to get to work.

While she was in the middle of folding, Martha opened the door and said, "We found the missing belongings of your predecessor, but they are a mess. Fold them so the gardener can take them to the police station."

Mercy followed, excited she would see her sister's belongings.

On the outside picnic table were two garbage bags. Off to the side were several empty boxes. The housekeeper motioned to them and said, "Pack them into the boxes so they can leave here in ten minutes." She walked back inside.

Not sure she could be done in the ten minutes Mercy had been given, wishing she had much longer to enjoy reconnecting with her sister, she was glad to have even this small moment of bonding.

Mercy opened up the first bag and pulled out clothes. She folded several pairs of jeans, a couple capris, two pairs of yoga pants and one pretty dress. She packed everything away in a box. In the bag, under the clothes, she found a collection of shoes and socks. She placed them at the bottom of the second box and opened the second bag to find more generic clothes, a heavy sweater and a jacket. She checked all the pockets but found nothing and realized the housekeeper had likely checked everything before placing them into the bags.

Disappointed and feeling rushed, she packed up the rest of the second bag. There was nothing personal of any kind in this assortment. These clothes could've belonged to anybody. There wasn't even a certain style here; they were all just clothes. Nothing that said they belonged to her sister, nothing that reminded her of her sister. Then it had been twelve years, so how would Mercy know? These clothes could have been her sister's. As she shook out the garbage bag, a small toiletry bag fell to the ground. She opened it and saw a hairbrush, a few items of makeup and a toothbrush and toothpaste.

Feeling bereft, heartbroken, and disappointed at not finding more, she closed the tops of the boxes as the gardener arrived. She folded up the garbage bags and said, "These two boxes are all I was handed of the maid's belongings."

"It's all there?" He gave her a sharp look, picked up both boxes and walked away.

She grabbed the two empty garbage bags and headed inside to the kitchen. Was it her imagination or did the chef shift his gaze away from her and back to his food? Had he been watching her out the window? This place was getting to her with its deep dark foreboding shadows and the constant sense of being under surveillance. Of course last night's visitor had to be the worst of it.

She put away the garbage bags and returned to the laundry. There she tried to catch up so she could still attempt to meet her regimented timeframe. She knew the housekeeper wouldn't give Mercy any extra time for the extra job done. Instead, she was expected to go faster and get it all done regardless.

And she made the effort to speed things up before lunchtime came around, but she was more tired than ever. She also needed something more substantial than additional servings of bread.

In the kitchen she found a new assistant to the kitchen staff. "Can I have something for lunch instead of sandwiches?" Mercy asked.

The guy looked at her in surprise. "Of course. What would you like?"

She shrugged. "Something that's not white bread. I'm very low on protein and veggies at the moment."

He smiled, opened the fridge and pulled out a big salad. Beside it was a plate of dates and another plate of sliced ham. He made her a big salad with all of the above.

She smiled with joy. "That looks delightful."

He handed her a knife and fork. She smiled again and stepped out to the little eating area as the door was closing behind her. He caught the door before it closed. "You don't have to eat out there all alone, you know?"

She glanced back. "I was told I was allowed to eat here."

He shook his head. "You can sit at the end of the dining room."

She glanced around the corner to the massive room where the owner sat sitting at the far end, paperwork everywhere, and shook her head. "No. I don't think I'd be welcome there but thanks." She gave a quick smile and stepped back outside, sitting down to enjoy her lunch.

She wondered how the kitchen assistant could be so opposite to everybody else in this place. It *was* the first time she'd met him. Had he been here before? Maybe not. She'd ask when she went back in. If he was new, they hadn't beaten that friendliness out of him yet.

With her only half-joking thought still in her head, she worked her way through the salad, loving every bite. Such a lovely change to have fresh food.

As she finished the last bite, she heard a sound around the corner of the house. Thinking it might be the gardener again, she stood up and collected her plate and cutlery, casually walking to the end of the patio as if to look out at the view.

Instead it was one of the security men, digging up the line. She glanced at him and frowned. "I don't think the gardener will like what you're doing," she joked.

He gave her a hard glance. "It won't matter if he likes it or not." He motioned toward the inside of the kitchen. "You shouldn't be here."

She held up her plate and with a touch of defiance said, "I just had my lunch."

"You're new here," he said quietly. "Are you nuts? You're not to see or watch or interact in any way with the rest of the property."

Her shoulders slumped. She had been given that lecture on her first day, but she'd been so excited and secure in the position and so full of hope of finding information about her sister that she'd glossed over how absolutely final the lecture had intended to be. She nodded. "I keep forgetting," she confessed.

"Head inside then before you get into trouble."

With a grateful smile she turned and walked back in. "That's two today," she murmured to herself.

Inside she rinsed her plate and put it in the dishwasher. There was no sign of the younger, friendlier kitchen assistant. Now that was too bad. She'd have loved a piece of dessert. She knew her meals were included with her job, but that didn't give her free right to rummage through the fridge.

She'd taken for granted her freedoms—when she had her own place to go to she could eat when she wanted to. Do what she wanted to and when she wanted to. Here these people made a science of making sure she ate only when and what she was given. If she wanted something more, she doubted it would be granted.

She walked to the far side, to the kitchen storage closet where her schedule was, and took note of where she was heading next.

MICHAEL DROVE OUT of the estate without looking back. If they'd handed over the clothing, then nothing was worth looking at. Still, he'd take it all to the police station as ordered.

And would continue to look around the estate.

He knew the commander wanted an update. But, if Michael hated one thing, that was to have nothing to show for his time. Except someone was a little too interested in the new maid for his liking. She was an innocent in all this. Misguided, perhaps, in her search for answers but still innocent.

He had to find a way to convince her to leave before more trouble found her.

Meanwhile, the security line remained broken, and the repairmen frantically tried to fix it. Michael had been watching for an opportunity to sabotage it further, but the security guards had been doubled. Michael didn't dare do anything that would put the new maid in danger, and Michael and Mercy were the only two unknowns on the estate. If Michael continued with his sabotage of the security system, then the owner would regard Michael and Mercy as the two most likely culprits. Michael was fine if the owner took a closer look at him. But Michael would be damned if he would let the owner hurt another innocent woman.

Chapter 6

THE REST OF the afternoon went by fast as nobody said a word to Mercy. But she assumed they all spoke about her. Anytime she saw someone, they sent a narrow gaze in her direction, assessing, wondering what she was up to. She understood she was getting more paranoid by the minute, but, by the time dinnertime rolled around, it was all she could do to contemplate food. Because, for the first time, she wondered if maybe she should run away in the middle of the night.

If that set off some alert within the security system, she'd get promptly stopped. Her stomach was in knots. She no longer had any sense of calm or of *I can do this*; she needed to get out. She couldn't blame this on her overwrought nerves as she'd never been the nervous high-strung female type. So it was very odd to see herself in that role now.

She put away the last of the cleaning supplies, stood the vacuum in the far corner and, with a last look around, closed the kitchen closet door. She found Martha studying her. Mercy raised an eyebrow and said, "I think I got everything done."

Martha nodded. "You look tired." And said it not in an empathetic way. More accusing. Judgmental.

Keeping everything inside, it was all she could do to not

scream at her and say, "Of course I'm tired. Anybody would be with the schedule you put me through." Instead she bit back any retorts and nodded. "I am actually."

"Well, get some dinner and rest up." As she walked away, she glanced back and said, "Do you have plans?"

"Plans?" Maybe she was so tired she didn't get the question, but it seemed something was hidden in Martha's question.

Martha nodded. "Are you going out anywhere tonight?"

"Maybe for a walk again."

"Okay. Don't be late. The security gates close at 10:00 p.m."

"Good to know. Thank you."

Because it was dinnertime, and she was expected to go for a meal, she headed in the direction of the kitchen. Before she got there, she glanced back. Sure enough Martha was still there, phone in her hand, talking, but her gaze was on Mercy. She slipped into the kitchen to find a little more chaos than normal.

The same chef's assistant she'd spoken to earlier smiled at her, pointed and immediately scooped up a plate that had been set off to the side. "This is for you."

She stared down at the roast beef, mashed potatoes, and hot steamed vegetables with relief. "Thank you," she said warmly.

He pointed to a corner of the kitchen where there was a small table for two. "Sit over there. It'll be more pleasant for you than outside in the muggy heat."

Obediently, she took her place at the table and sat down with her back to the kitchen staff. The last thing she wanted to do was watch them while they watched her. She knew they couldn't be watching her with all the work they had to do, but it still felt like they were.

She ate slowly, not happy she was so tired. It wasn't normal for her. Usually she was a high-energy individual. And, yes, the physical work here was taxing, but it shouldn't be *that* bad. She lifted a hand and rubbed her forehead. She was feeling rough enough, maybe she needed to lie down. And how wrong was it that a healthy twenty-seven-year-old woman had to go lie down after doing housework?

She polished off her meal, wishing she could have more roast beef but not wanting to draw any more attention to herself by asking. She stood and carried her plate to the dishwasher.

The same young man smiled, grabbed the plate from her and said, "I'll take that."

She gave him a brief smile. "It was delicious, thank you."

But he'd already turned away and stacked the dishes in the dishwasher. Everybody else appeared to be busy too.

She hadn't been offered any dessert, so she presumed that was all she would get. Then again that should be more than enough. She left the kitchen and went up to her room, thinking about a store not too far away. She could always walk down there and pick up some snacks to keep in her room. It would also get her out of here for a while. She only had a small bag of personal items with her because she wore a uniform every day. She had planned to grab some clothes from her apartment, but she hadn't had the energy to get them.

She did have her wheels, parked on the side of the garage.

She'd been planning on buying a new vehicle before her sister's death, but that had put everything on the back burner. And the old small car was perfect for her role as the maid.

Sitting on the bed, she contemplated her next step. Her nerves had calmed down, but, at the same time, she didn't think she would be safe staying here for much longer, and, if that was the case, why stay here at all?

Martha's question about whether Mercy was going out tonight was unnerving too. She only had the one bag, but it would be hard to sneak out with it and not have somebody know. She did have a very large purse. She glanced around at the stuff she'd used and the clothing she'd brought but didn't need. She quickly packed several books and reduced her belongings down to the bare necessities.

With the rest packed into her purse and a small plastic bag, she walked downstairs and outside to her car. She pulled out of the large parking space and headed toward the closest grocery store. As it had a coffee shop attached, she went there first and ordered a latte. Pulling out her laptop, she sat down in one of the corners and settled in to some alone time.

She went to her social media accounts to see if there was any word of her sister. There was nothing. As she enjoyed her coffee, catching up on the world news, an email came in. She clicked on it, not knowing who the sender was. The message was clear.

Don't return home tonight. Michael.

She stared at it, puzzled, not even sure who Michael was. Did somebody realize she was here right now? Had she been followed from the estate? If so, then that person came from the estate too. Surely he could have told her face-to-face. Why didn't he? And how had he gotten her email address?

She slammed her computer closed and sat trembling inside. She picked up her latte and held it close, trying to gain comfort from the drink.

She knew the security people watched her inside the house. How far outside on the property—and beyond—could they watch her? She quickly opened her laptop and hit Reply, typing, *Why? Who are you? Why can't you tell me this to my face?* She glanced around the small coffee shop, hating to think somebody had followed her. Was sitting in here right now.

She'd driven her car from the estate and headed here, not giving a thought that she might be followed, that anybody from the estate might've understood where she was going. Why would they care? She hadn't done anything wrong. She hadn't even gotten her nose in anybody's business by asking too many questions. She had worked damn hard, and yet what did she get? Everywhere she turned, people were telling her what to do—to mind her own business or to work harder or, like now, to not return.

Why the warning? Things were getting more and more shadowy instead of giving her the clarity she craved.

A reply was flashing on her screen. She read it aloud, under her breath, "*You know who I am. I only want to help.*"

She rested her fingers on the keyboard and began typing.

If you want to help, tell me what's wrong at that place.

She wondered at her common sense and her need for this conversation with this nut job, even if he was trying to help. But she couldn't resist hitting the Send button. When the answer came a few minutes later, she stared at it in pain.

Your sister was murdered as was someone else. Is that not

enough for you?

So Michael was the gardener. Her fingers were already working the keyboard. She asked him where he was right now. If it was dangerous for her, it had to be doubly dangerous for him. Particularly if he was trying to find answers. If so, what had he found out, she wanted to know. She needed to know what had happened to her sister.

She waited and waited, but there was no answer. Frustrated, she sat back and studied the little coffee shop, drank a little more of her coffee and enjoyed the freedom of being away from the oppressive air of the estate. When she'd finally finished her cup, she rose, tossed the empty paper cup in the garbage, picked up her laptop, checking once more to make sure Michael hadn't answered, shut it down and put it away.

She checked her phone for messages. It looked like Michael wouldn't give any more answers to her questions. Frustrated, and out of sorts, she walked to the grocery store. She bought fresh fruits, some granola bars, and a package of black licorice—a childhood treat she allowed herself every once in a while. At the checkout, she paid and left. As she approached her car, bag in hand, she caught sight of something she didn't like one bit.

She stared at the gardener, leaning against her car, and frowned. "So you're Michael."

His piercing blue eyes studied her for a long moment before he nodded.

Relief coursed through her. "Why didn't you say so? That first email terrified me."

"I THOUGHT YOU'D know it was me," Michael said, studying her curiously. "Who else would it be?"

Her disgusted look made him want to smile. But the words out of her mouth surprised him.

"I know you think I look like a completely stupid innocent who's not aware of the dangers of the world, but you couldn't be more wrong."

"Really? You work for a marketing company. That hardly gives you experience in the evil world of serial killers and drug cartels. Or bankrolling terrorists."

She froze. "Is that what you think happened to Anna? She was involved with drugs when I knew her but small time. I have no idea what she was into since."

"It's a little late to be worried about her fate now."

She winced. "That's not fair. She took off and never came back. I spent years looking for her. And, when I found her a few years ago, I asked her to have coffee with me. But she didn't want anything to do with me. I tried to keep tabs on her, sending her emails. I kept the door open in case she ever wanted to walk through it again. But ..."

His voice softened. "But she never got the chance to."

Mercy nodded. "Did you happen to look through her things?"

"The stuff I saw didn't prove they were hers."

Mercy nodded. "That's what I thought. And that's not normal. There should've been something. I did find a notebook though."

He straightened abruptly, glanced around the area, motioned at the coffee shop and said, "Come on. Let's have coffee."

She frowned. "I just had coffee. That's where I was when you emailed me."

But he wouldn't take no for an answer. Instead, he gently grabbed her by the elbow and nudged her toward the coffee shop.

He ordered two coffees and led her to the table in the farthest corner. Realizing nobody was around so they could not be overheard, she sat down facing the room. She studied all the other patrons, wondering still if it was safe.

He nudged the ceramic coffee cup toward her and said, "This is for you."

She nodded. "Why are you there if it's that dangerous?" He studied her quietly but didn't say a word, and she got it. "You're there to find out something." She narrowed her gaze and studied his jaw and full head of hair. "Are you undercover? A cop?"

His laconic answer came. "Yes. No."

Shrewdly she said, "Undercover, yes, but a different division."

He shrugged. "We're on the same side. That's all that matters."

"Fine, we're on the same side. We both want to get answers as to what happened to my sister and the last gardener."

Michael nodded.

She gently swirled the contents of her cup. He watched her study the beautiful heart in the center. It made him feel good when she smiled.

Then she sat back with a heavy sigh. "It's been hard, day after day, going through the motions, working to keep up to their nightmarish schedule and all they expect of me while knowing someone took my sister's life. Knowing my hands are cleaning, wiping across the same walls as my sister's hands did. Then I vacuum, holding the vacuum where her hands used to grasp it before me."

He watched as tears welled up in the corners of her eyes. She brushed them away impatiently.

He agreed. The time for tears were well past. Now she needed enough anger to get through the process of getting answers. "What notebook?"

Startled, she glanced at him, reached into her purse and pulled out the small notebook she'd found. She handed it over.

Michael studied it. The front page had Anna's name and a number. He considered the number but didn't recognize it. He glanced over at Anna's sister and asked, "Do you know this number?"

Mercy shook her head. "No. It might be her phone number. I haven't tried it."

He pulled out his phone and punched in the numbers. He waited, and sure enough a pre-recorded answer came on.

"Hi, you've reached Anna. Sorry I can't come to the phone right now."

He hit the Stop button. "It's her phone number. It went straight to her voice mail."

"Of course it did. She's dead," Mercy said brusquely. "But why was there no phone found?"

"Whoever killed her probably took it and smashed it."

"That's possible." Mercy raised an eyebrow but didn't ask further.

For which he was grateful.

She smiled. "I would be happy to think she was busy and couldn't come to the phone right now. It would be nice to think she had a life outside of that nasty place. I hate to think she was alone, working and going nowhere in a dungeon like that." Then she frowned. "Who was Sammy? Maybe he was into drugs?"

Michael shook his head. "No. I knew Sammy. He wasn't into drugs."

He gave her a bland look as she stared at him in surprise. Then she leaned forward. "It's the reason you took the job. Same as I did. You came to find answers."

He gave her a clipped nod. "But I haven't found anything yet. Where did you find Anna's notebook?" He pulled out his cell phone and took several images of the pages of writing.

"Behind the bathroom medicine cabinet," she answered.

His eyebrows rose. "*Hmm*." He quickly flipped through the pages again. "Why would she hide it? Is something major in here?"

"She mentions crates of guns being unloaded on the property," she confessed, her voice barely above a whisper, her fingers clutching her coffee cup until her knuckles turned white. "And she was unsure about trusting Sammy but loved him and hoped she was making the right decision."

His gaze locked on hers as if looking for confirmation. Then he quickly flipped through the notebook until he got to the pertinent page. Most of the book was empty, but, as she watched Michael, he snapped a photo of every page that had writing. He flipped to the back of the notebook. "Too bad there isn't more."

"It's got to be why they were killed. They must have been

seen or mentioned the guns to the wrong person."

"It's possible. The notes do confirm something shady is going on," Michael said quietly.

"I'm hoping she wasn't involved, but I'm not kidding when I say I knew nothing about her life. She wouldn't let us in ever again."

"Sammy wouldn't have left until he got to the bottom of this, so I'm presuming he was close if he and Anna were making plans to leave." He switched on his cell phone and typed out a message to Levi. "I'm sending these pages off to be analyzed," he told Mercy.

"I wish I could ask someone here about her. All I've been told is to watch myself, to stay away from people and to not talk." She shook her head. "I'd be starving if it wasn't for the one young cook in the kitchen. He's been nice."

"Your room and board is included with your wages?"

She nodded. "And, speaking of which, I need to be back before ten o'clock as they lock the gates." She glanced at her watch. "It's nine-thirty already."

"Don't return," he said suddenly. He didn't know how to convince her to leave, but he had to try. It was too damn dangerous.

She glanced up at him. "I know it's bad, but is it that bad?"

"Who was that at your door last night?"

She winced. "They never knocked," she said slowly. "I have no idea who it was. I figured maybe they'd hired somebody new, and they had the room next to mine, but I think they stood outside my door the entire time."

"He did."

She leaned forward. "You saw him? Who was it?"

He shook his head. "I saw the shadow through the window in the hallway, standing at your door for a long time. Then he left, and you turned on the light right afterward."

"I saw you watching me while he was outside my door." She studied him for a long moment. "I wondered if you were watching me or watching him. Then I couldn't help but wonder if the two of you were working together."

He stared at her, both eyebrows shooting toward his hairline. "I had nothing to do with it. Unfortunately I couldn't see who it was."

"It goes along with all the other shit happening throughout the day."

"Like?"

She quickly explained, and he went silent, considering this new information.

Chapter 7

MERCY THOUGHT ABOUT what he had said. She thought about the look in his eyes, the tone of his voice, and held a heartfelt belief that what he had said was what she needed to hear. She dropped her gaze to study the tabletop. "I have to go back. I made a promise to my sister, to myself. I promised I would get to the bottom of this, and I would find out what happened."

He picked up her hand. She stared at his suntanned, calloused fingers as they gently stroked her soft white hand.

"And you are doing it. But you should be doing it in a way that doesn't put you in danger," Michael said. "And you won't know how much danger exists until it's too late. Two people have already been murdered. For all I know, other staff members have disappeared as well. The detectives are looking into both murders. We have to give them a chance to do their job."

"Then you should leave too," she said. "Sammy was there before you. For all the owner knows, you're involved in whatever Sammy was involved in too."

"Same for you as one of the two new hires."

She studied the hard glint in his gaze. "But I don't know anything about Mr. Freeman. And nobody at the estate knows

I'm Anna's sister. Nobody talks to me about either of the dead employees. I can't ask questions. I can't do anything. The minute I do, I'm told to be quiet and to do my job." She turned her gaze to study her coffee cup. "Did my sister ever get time off? Did she ever come here to relax, just to get away? Was that job nothing but hell for her?"

"I'm hoping she found something enjoyable in life with Sammy."

"What was he like?"

"Full of fun, full of laughter. He was always playing catch-up," he said abruptly. "Capable, determined to be better. Sometimes he needed help where the rest of us didn't, but he was funny. He was heartwarming and good-natured."

"Then I'm happy for her. If she found somebody like that, then it's a whole lot better than what she left home with."

"Explain?"

Mercy shrugged and settled back into the comfortable chair. "She took off with a local bad boy. He ran with gangs, rode a bike, did drugs, sold drugs. He was suspected of pimping out high school girls." She shook her head. "We did everything we could to stop her, to save her, but she wouldn't listen to us."

"She had a child."

Mercy stared at him, her jaw dropping. She leaned forward and hissed, "What? How do you know? Where is the child?"

He shook his head. "I ran her numbers, license plate, and talked to a cop friend of mine," he said. "Years ago she gave it up for adoption."

Mercy sat back up, stunned by the news. "Giving her child up for adoption is something I can see her doing. It was likely much better for the child at the time." Her heart leaped and soared at the thought of a child, a piece of her sister still on the planet. "Is there a way to find out the details on the adoption?"

He shook his head. "Not until the child's eighteen. Some states allow parents to post notices on websites that they're looking for the child, but, more often than not, it has to be the child who goes looking for the parents."

"Is it a boy or girl?"

He tilted his head, and his lips came up on one side. "A boy."

"Can you tell me when he was born?"

"Eleven years ago."

"Does he have a name?"

He shook his head. "I don't know those details."

She nodded; she couldn't imagine. Thank God, her mother wasn't alive to hear this. Her mother would have been horrified to hear Anna had given up her son. Mercy couldn't do anything about it at this point, except hope that, down the road, the boy went looking for his family. "Maybe it's a good thing my mother is gone. The news would have broken her heart all over again."

"Wait and see. Nothing can be done to contact him for a lot of years yet."

She nodded. "And that's just as hard to deal with. My mother would have taken the child in. No matter the problem with Anna, we would've taken them both in, had we known."

"Maybe she didn't have a choice. Maybe she thought she

could keep it and raise it and then realized, in the end, there was no other way."

"He's not even mentioned in the journal," Mercy said suddenly. "Surely if Anna knew she would die or was in danger, she'd spare a thought for the child she walked away from."

"A lot of women walk away, and it's permanent. They shove it deep inside. They don't think about it. For other women, when they put up their child for adoption, it haunts them daily. There's no way to know."

Mercy hated to think it had been easy for her sister to walk away, even though Anna had not had an easy life and had a much harder death. She must have been terrified at the end. And that brought Mercy back to the man who died at her sister's side. "She must have spent some nights at Sammy's place. Was there any sign left of her or him when you moved in?"

"No. Everything had been cleaned out."

"Did you look behind the medicine cabinet?"

"I tried, but mine is bolted in. What made you decide to look there?"

"I was brushing my teeth and noticed it was a little off. When I straightened it, it was lose, easy to pull out. They are supposed to be screwed in for safety."

"She probably removed the screws, intended to replace them, but they wouldn't hold in the dry wall without anchors. I still think you shouldn't return again."

"And I think I have to. If you're staying, then we're both in danger. If one of us leaves, it puts the other one in more danger."

He studied her for a long moment. "I can take care of myself."

She winced. "Of course you can. I, on the other hand, am a complete dunce about any kind of self-defense. However, I know how to keep my head down and continue working."

"Yet, you're tired," he said abruptly.

"I am," she admitted. "It's not the easiest of jobs. At the same time, there was something almost welcoming about following my sister's path."

"As long as you don't follow it all the way to the same end," he reminded her. He glanced at his watch and said, "We're out of time. We have fifteen minutes before the gate closes."

She bolted to her feet. "Oh, my God. They won't let either of us in after that."

The two walked outside and hopped into his truck. As it was, they pulled into the gates moments before the security triggered them to lock down at 10:00 p.m.

Once inside the grounds, he parked close to his garage apartment. She opened the truck door and hopped out with her grocery bag. "I'm an idiot. I left my car back there," she wailed.

"I'll take you back in the morning. We'll pick it up."

She thought about that and frowned. "When do the gates open?"

"Six o'clock."

She nodded with relief. "I don't start work until seven, so that would work. And my car should be fine in the coffee shop parking lot."

He smiled. "It'll be fine."

"Good night. And thanks for looking after me." His smile surprised her. She didn't think he gave them too often. She hated to admit it, but she looked forward to each and every one of them.

Knowing she was late—and probably being watched—she raced to the door, happy to find it was still unlocked. She didn't know if the individual buildings were locked down at the same time or not. As long as she could get in, then it was all good.

As she entered, Martha stepped out from the corner. Her face was dark, a frown taking over most of her features. "You're late," she snapped.

Mercy's surprise was genuine. "I didn't realize there was a curfew. You told me the gates close at ten but didn't say anything about the buildings or that I had to be in my room," she said, puzzled. "I haven't been sleeping all that well. I was thinking it would be nice to walk around in the evening."

Martha shook her head. "Nobody is allowed outside after 10:00 p.m."

Wondering what the hell was going on and why such a rule was necessary, Mercy said, "Okay. I didn't realize that part." She shifted her bag to her other hand and started toward the stairs. "I didn't mean to break any rules."

"Where's your car?"

Her back stiffened at Martha's harsh tone. "I left it at the grocery store. I was having coffee at the café and met Michael. When he told me how we had so little time to get back before the gates closed, I grabbed a ride with him rather than walking around back where my car was parked. I'll go in the morning and pick it up." Not waiting to hear Martha's response, Mercy quickly raced up the stairs. She unlocked the door to her room and rushed inside. After slamming the door behind her, she relocked it. Martha was strict, and she was also damn scary.

Mercy carried her bag to the bed and dropped it, kicking off her shoes. She turned on the light, walked to the window and opened the curtain. Instinctively she knew she'd see somebody watching her from the far side. And, sure enough, Michael leaned against the window inside his apartment on the other side of the yard. She gave him a small wave and unpacked the little bit of groceries she had. She had taken a lot of her belongings when she went out earlier and discovered she had left one of the bags in her car. So the fact was, she was half moved out already. On that odd note she quickly got ready for bed. She'd had lots of coffee though so was still awake.

As she made her way to her bed, she pulled the covers back and froze. She'd been making beds Martha's way all day inside the big house, but she hadn't remade her bed the same. She'd used a shortcut, almost out of defiance, after having made so many in the last few days. Had she automatically fixed hers to match the rest of the house? She stood up slightly and studied the bed. No. Definitely somebody had straightened it out.

She glanced around the room. Had anything else been disturbed? Unnerved and wary, she did a thorough search of her small room and bathroom. But, since she hadn't left much behind, outside of the bedding being straightened, she wasn't sure she could prove she'd had an evening visitor.

She walked to the window and stared at Michael. Her phone buzzed. Knowing it was him, yet she hadn't given him her number, she pulled it out and read the text. She quickly answered with

My room was searched.

How can you tell?

The bed has been made up differently.

She looked around the room as she waited for his response. What else had been done while she was gone? She thought about calling him, but was it possible her room had been bugged? Sharing this news with him over a phone call would also put him in trouble, and that was the last thing she wanted. This stuff was off the wall. It was making her hair stand up. She quickly texted him.

What if my room is bugged?

Her phone rang at the same time. She answered it, somehow knew it would be Michael.

"Get out. Get out now and stay out," Michael responded.

She stared in shock at her phone. "Why?" She wanted to say more, but what if someone was listening?

"Don't be a fool. Hasn't enough happened yet? Do you need the next thing to be bigger, worse than this?"

"I wondered why they'd do this, but there's nothing here to find."

Silence followed.

Until a text buzzed in her hand.

Get out now. Someone might be listening in.

Then she heard footsteps coming up the stairs. Shit.

MICHAEL WATCHED THROUGH the window, wishing she'd turn around and pack up the last of her stuff and sneak out. He knew the alarms would be set, and getting out might not be an easy thing, but considering the security system was on the blink, she might have a fair chance.

As he watched her at her bedroom window, once again he saw a flash of light at the ground floor landing, meaning someone was creeping upstairs. He quickly sent her a text, but she didn't answer. He watched as she walked to the bed, her shadowy form beyond the sheers. She sat heavily on her bed, the overhead light still on. It might be enough to send the shadow a beam of light under her main door.

He sent another text in warning. And watched anxiously as the shadow stopped once again at the top of the landing, courtesy of the window there. As far as Michael understood, there had been no new hires. So this hallway lurker was somebody who'd been on the estate for a long enough time to know where Mercy was and even what she was doing in that room. He could see her flash around the room as if packing up. He sure as hell hoped so. She clicked off the lamp. Instantly her room was in darkness.

He studied the drop outside her window, but there was no veranda, no small patio and no fire escape. She had no way to get out of there, at least not easily. As he prepared to race across the yard and come to her rescue, he watched the shadow slowly creep downstairs again. Unnerved, he wanted to smash the asshole's face to smithereens for tormenting her.

He watched as the light went out at the bottom of the stairs, and then the door next to those stairs opened. One of the security men came out, on a walkie-talkie. In essence he'd been checking that she was in her room. Seeing her light go off had confirmed she'd gone to bed.

Now that was creepy. Would they do the same for him?

He glanced around his room. He had a little bit more here than she did. His room had been checked within the first twenty-four hours of his arrival. They weren't taking any chances on the estate. But he hadn't brought anything suspicious with him and had worked hard to make sure he had nothing of any value either.

But he wasn't ready to pack up and leave. He had to figure out what happened to Sammy before he left. Failure was not an option. In larger estates, often a hierarchy existed within the staff, and sometimes the lower-tier staff members had to pay the higher-tier staff members to just stay out of their life. He hadn't been approached with a bribe like that, but he wouldn't put it past this place. Although, if the boss found out, they'd be sacked in a heartbeat.

He turned his attention back to the window and sent a text to Mercy.

The security guard checked to see that you were inside. He's now outside doing a perimeter walk.

The response came back almost instantly.

Okay. That makes sense.

Like hell. I wish you'd get out now.

I'm not leaving yet.

Then, damn it, when we get your car in the morning, make sure you leave nothing behind. You

won't be coming back.

He tossed his phone on the bed. He had to get her out of here. He hadn't heard or seen anything, but his instincts were screaming at him. If for any reason they found out who she was, she'd be dead in a heartbeat.

Sleep that night was hard to come by. He dozed in one-hour blocks, waking and checking to make sure all was well, and then sleeping again. When five o'clock rolled around, he was already up, sipping coffee. The gates would open at six, and he wanted to be on the road getting her out of here at five minutes past six. She was a mite too stubborn for him. But he understood loyalty.

He also understood the need to get answers. But she had to walk away and leave that for the pros. He sent her a text at six.

Are you ready?

To get my car, yes, but I'm coming back. I want answers.

I'll get the answers. You get to safety.

Going to get some breakfast.

He put away his phone. *Don't try any tricks, Mercy. These men are not to be fooled around with.* But he already knew she wouldn't cooperate.

Then he packed up the rest of his gear so it was all in one bag, loaded his laptop into his backpack, tossed it over his shoulder and walked out with the keys. He locked the apartment door behind him, set a trap to make sure he'd know if anybody had been in the apartment in his absence, then headed to his truck. He wasn't officially on duty until seven-thirty. He had lots of time to get her into town to her car and to get back.

He warmed up the truck and pulled it to the side of the house. When she didn't arrive, he sent her a quick text.

Engine's running.

She didn't come for the longest time. When he decided to find her himself, she came out, still munching on a piece of toast. She hopped in, bag in hand and shot him a grumpy look. "I need food, you know? So I made a piece of toast for the road."

"You could eat in town."

"Or I can eat on my way back," she muttered.

"You aren't going back."

"Of course I am," she said with spirit. "It makes perfect sense they'd be checking to ensure I was safe and sound last night."

He shot her a look of disbelief. "When they weren't checking to see if you were talking on the phone, sending messages, bringing over a visitor. ... They could be doing all kinds of things."

"You live in an ugly world, don't you? If that's what comes to mind ..."

"And you're not so innocent. Your sister was murdered. That should be enough to make you take major precautions."

"I am. But it's also enough for me to want answers."

On impulse, he drove past her car and headed to the police station.

"What the hell," she exclaimed. "Where are we going?"

"To talk to the detective. See if he has an update."

Her anger subsided. "Oh, that's a good idea."

They were glad when they arrived to find the detective getting out of his own vehicle. He raised an eyebrow at the sight of the two of them together. "I don't have much news," he warned.

"You have some?" Mercy asked eagerly.

"Not really. I finally got your sister's clothing, but there was nothing there. Her DNA was found on the toothbrush. I can give the items to you when our forensic team is done."

Crestfallen, she nodded. "I went through them too."

He looked at her. "What? How?"

Michael interjected. "That's one of the reasons I wanted to see you. She took her sister's place at the house. I want her out of there. It's getting dangerous. And I don't want to see her end up dead like her sister."

The detective swore when he heard what she'd done. "That's not smart. You're in the middle of our investigation, and I can't have that."

She jutted her chin out at both men. "I did what I had to do. To get answers. And nobody else has gotten them for me."

The detective turned to Michael. "How dangerous is it?"

Michael shrugged. "There hasn't been anything specific, but every night they check to ensure she's locked into her room." Michael looked at her. "Plus she feels like she's being watched all the time, and she's always warned to stick to herself and to not talk to anybody else."

The detective faced her. "Is that true?"

She nodded. "But it's not that bad yet. I was scared when

I heard footsteps coming up the stairs. Nobody knocked. But knowing a man stood outside the door scared me. I understand now though. The security system's all goofy. It makes sense for the guards to confirm if I'm inside or out."

Michael glared at her. "Honestly?"

The cop stared at her in surprise. "Surely you're not that naive."

She frowned at them both. "No, I'm not."

Chapter 8

IN FACT MERCY wasn't naive at all. "I'm not making too big a deal out of it. And I did go through my sister's belongings as I packed them up for you. But I didn't find anything personal. However, I did find a notebook." She turned to Michael. "Did you bring it?"

He pulled it from his back pocket and handed it to the detective.

"It was my sister's. I found it behind the medicine cabinet in my room."

He glanced at her. "What's in it?"

"She talks about a new boyfriend but doesn't mention much about the people she worked with. She doesn't leave any names. She was a little bit suspicious and afraid she was being watched." Mercy took a deep breath, knowing the next bit would surprise him. "She saw crates of guns being unloaded."

Flipping through the pages, the detective whistled. "That's huge."

"I can't believe they'd do anything so stupid as to kill a second maid so quickly," she protested.

"Who said they'd kill you?" Michael argued. "Even if they did, what if they made you disappear? What if they told the detective here how you found the job too hard and ran off in tears?"

The detective added, "That's not unusual. You disappear into the streets, and nobody would know anything about you."

She shook her head. "This isn't medieval times. There has to be some way to get the information we need."

"How's the security on the place?"

"It would be a hell of a lot better if Michael would stop sabotaging the lines," she said with spirit.

Michael stared at her, his eyes dark, flat. "It was necessary," he said.

"Oh, I don't doubt it," she said with a smile. "But don't tell me how I don't notice things."

"If you do return …" the detective said, holding up the notebook, "given that you found this already, what else do you think you'd find?"

"I have no idea," she said. "But I won't know unless I look again."

The detective shook his head. "Think about it. These men have killed twice. Nothing will stop them from killing a third time. If you become too nosy, too suspicious, or *too* anything else, they'd make sure you're not around to prove the first two murders."

"And yet, it'd be suspicious to have another person disappear from the estate."

"Only if they weren't the ones who made you *disappear*." Michael's voice was hard as he added, "They are planning something."

The detective's tone sharpened. "What and when?"

Michael gave a half smile. "You'll know when I find out.

So far lots of meetings are behind closed doors with lots of people coming and going, plus activity in the lower levels."

"Lower levels?" Mercy repeated. "I know about the wine cellar, but that's all." Yet the place was huge, so it was possible.

He nodded. "Two full floors are below the main floor. One is set up as a big meeting room with a separate entrance and exit I haven't found yet. The other floor is for a big wine cellar and storage room and some warehouse space."

"Any idea what's stored there?"

Michael sent a sideways glance at the cop. "I suspected drugs but, after seeing the notebook, likely guns or both. Yet there is an air of something happening, but I have no idea what's going on. If we're lucky, it'll be a new shipment coming in."

"Can you get down there to see?"

"Maybe. Depends what comes. They might need extra muscles. I don't know that I can get pictures though."

Mercy stepped back and listened as the two men discussed it. "I might be able to clean down there," she said suddenly.

Both men looked at her and frowned.

She rushed into saying, "I've been sent to the cellar to get some wine. Just once though."

"Did you see what else was down there?" the detective asked.

She shook her head. "It's very dim, and it's huge."

"Is it big enough to store guns?" the detective asked. "Although he'd be foolish to keep everything on-site."

"If he didn't keep it on-site, it's hard to watch over it," Michael reminded him.

Mercy glanced at her watch. "We have to get my car and return to the estate. If anything happens, or if I feel any uneasiness, I'll walk straight out. I'll grab my stuff and go to my car. The gates will be open until 10:00 p.m. tonight. I can leave at any time. But, if that meeting *is* happening, you'll need me to get photos of people coming and going."

Michael shook his head. "Not photos. If I'm chauffeuring, I can set up a camera in the car. We'll take photos of everyone getting in and out of my vehicle."

She brightened. "That's ingenious."

He snorted. "It's what I do."

She gave him a beaming smile. "Good. I'm glad to hear that."

In truth, she didn't know what to think about him. That he took her to the police station and was trying to convince her not to return said a lot about how caring he was. It was good to know Michael was with her there. That he knew who she was and why she was there. Although she was in danger, having him close made her feel more secure. Maybe that wasn't a good thing. She certainly didn't want to get into any issues, like her sister had, but Mercy was already involved.

People who remembered her sister would say the way she died was to be expected. But her sister hadn't been all bad. It was easy to judge people. Sometimes people lost track of who someone was on the inside.

Unfortunately Sammy and her sister were gone. All Mercy could do was surmise what might happen at this point and consider who on the estate was likely involved. She hated to say it, but she needed the police to find out what was going on. In whatever way that would be. While staying and working at the estate made her unhappy, she wasn't quite ready to give up her post. She had this sense that she could do more, even though she'd tried everything she knew. Maybe she could talk to more people, like the nice kitchen assistant. But she didn't know what his schedule was. "I have to get back. I don't dare be late for work."

She watched as the two men exchanged glances; then the detective gave a hard nod.

"You can return, but you have stay in touch. Just send me a simple text check in at 9pm tonight and again in the morning." He glared at her and added, "And before you say something stupid, remember what happened to your sister." He pulled out two business cards.

She winced. "That's hardly fair."

"There's nothing fair about any of this," Michael retorted. He took the cards the detective offered, giving one to Mercy. "Send him a text and also one to me." Before they left the detective's office, he grabbed a pen off the desk and quickly wrote down his name and phone number on a card and handed it back to the detective. "She already has my cell phone number," he said by way of explanation. The detective stood. "I can't force you to stay away," he said, turning back toward her, "but everything inside of me says you shouldn't return."

She nodded. "Today I'll go. Then I'll see."

Back in the truck, she glanced at Michael's expression. "I'll be careful, you know? I don't have a death wish."

He snorted. "Apparently you do. You're going back."

"Maybe I can find something useful," she argued.

"Yeah, like what?"

She was at a loss for an answer. She hated to feel useless. "Talk to somebody to find out any information."

"And maybe you won't find out anything."

"I found the notebook. I'll stay today, maybe overnight, and then I'll get out."

As they pulled into the parking lot beside her car, before she could get out, he grabbed her hand so she couldn't escape. "Promise?"

She sighed. "If you're sure I'm in that much trouble, I promise."

He nodded. "I'll hold you to it. That means you will be coming out tomorrow morning at the latest. I'd rather have you leave tonight."

"Why do you think they're making sure I'm in my room?" she asked.

He peered out the windshield. "Logic suggests they don't want you to see or hear something they're doing."

"But the doors are not locked from the outside. There's nothing to stop me from leaving or going out to look around to see what they're doing."

He studied her face for a moment. "Unless they have cameras or alarms at your bedroom door. I thought your room might be bugged too." He studied her face for a long moment. "How do you sleep there?"

"I'm exhausted, so I sleep like a log," she admitted.

He nodded as if he expected that answer.

"To be expected. You work hard. Too hard." He settled back. "Good. Be careful. I don't want you falling sick."

HE WAITED UNTIL she got into her car, his mind worrying, fussing. What he had said was true. Sammy might've been a lot of things, but he'd have been very aware of any surrounding dangers. His instincts were second to none. Sure, Michael didn't know what had ended Sammy's life, but Michael would know soon enough. He'd find out.

He always kept his blinds closed, his lights off behind the curtains. Last night he'd sat up with his binoculars to see what was going on outside. And definitely something was going on. Two vehicles had been let in at midnight of the previous night, like he had told the detective earlier. They were still inside the triple garage at the house. A garage he suspected he wouldn't be allowed anywhere close to. That was okay. Because as long as he wasn't allowed someplace, that was where he wanted to be, and he'd get in on his own time.

But he had to make sure Mercy would be safe too. He understood her loyalty. He understood her need for answers. But he wanted her to get the hell away. He had her promise of only one more night. Now, maybe, if he was lucky, he'd get her out of here before nightfall. Then he could go walking about the estate, checking out a few things.

He drove back to the estate, making sure he was a car or two behind her. She drove between the gates and parked in her usual spot. He knew they'd already been noticed. He parked in his spot, hopped out and walked up to his apartment. Nothing had been disturbed. That went with his theory it was either bugged or they had a camera he hadn't found, which pissed him off. He'd checked the place out thoroughly when he had first arrived; now he fully intended to give the place a clean sweep again.

When done, he checked his watch. It was time to go. Good or bad, his day as a chauffeur and gardener had started. He grabbed an apple from his fridge with a chunk of cheese, opened the door and headed downstairs. As soon as he exited, Bruce, the head of security and his boss, stood beside him.

Michael glanced at him and asked, "What can I do for you?"

"I'd like to know where you and the maid were this morning," Bruce said in a hard voice.

Michael gave a casual shrug. "We ran into each other at a coffee shop last night. She hadn't been feeling well, and it was late, so she hitched a ride with me. I drove her to get her car this morning."

Bruce rolled his eyes and nodded. "Work in the yard today. Stay away from the garages and stick to the house, please. We'll have a lot of security as we fix the lines."

Michael nodded. "Sure, no problem." He took a big bite of his apple and headed to the garden. Just what he had expected. All kinds of stuff going on. Now he had to figure out what it was.

Chapter 9

M ERCY WALKED INTO the main house, looking for breakfast. She was starving again. That little bit of toast earlier had long been used up. With the amount of work she'd been doing, she was unsure if anything could fill her. In the kitchen, she found the chef prepping breakfast.

He lifted his gaze. "I'll have a plate for you in a few minutes. Go sit outside."

She nodded and grabbed a cup of coffee. Muffins were off to the side in a basket. She took one of those and stepped onto the veranda. She hoped the chef would bring her a big plate of food, and she could save the muffin for later. But, when she looked at the muffin, she realized how hungry she was. She finished it off in about five bites. She had no butter to go with it because she'd felt like she'd snatched it instead of being allowed it.

As she finished, the young guy she'd met the day before stepped out, only this time he was minus the smile. Without saying a word, he gave her a plate of eggs, sausage, and hash browns.

She smiled in relief. "Thank you," she said. "I'm always hungry here."

He shook his head and patted her shoulder. "We're not

supposed to be too friendly but no need to starve. I'll bring the toast in a minute."

Realizing from his words and manner he'd likely been chastised by Martha, like Mercy had, she gave him a quiet smile. "Well, the friendliness and extra food are appreciated. Thank you."

He disappeared, and she dug in. It was a little hot outside, but it wasn't too bad.

As she ate, she could hear voices approaching. This was a tiny little staff patio. She didn't think anybody who worked inside the house took advantage of this. It was one of the reasons she liked to sit here. She could hear snippets of the conversation from those working outside.

"We've searched the lines all through the kitchen. There are no breaks, no tampering."

"We have to keep searching. If we can't get this going, we'll have to run new lines. It needs to be done by noon today."

"Got it."

"Robert," the first man said, "I'm not joking. Make sure it's done by noon. Or else. Got that?"

She assumed it was Robert who answered, "We'll do our best," his voice a little nervous. Too bad she couldn't see his face.

"No, that's not good enough," the other man said, his voice hardening a bit. "We need it done fast. We have things on tap that can't go forward until we get the security system up and running."

"Understood."

The voices disappeared. She thought she heard one man

still working on the side of the house.

Then the same young assistant came back out with a plate of toast. In his other hand he held a small plate with several muffins. He put them both down beside her. "If you don't eat the muffins right now, you can always save them for when you take a break."

She glanced up at him. "I haven't been allowed to take any breaks."

He nodded. "The place is touchy right now. Hang in there. You'll be fine."

At his words, she settled back and enjoyed her breakfast.

There was something very comforting about plain hot buttered toast after eating a meal. She packed the muffins in several napkins before putting them in each of her pockets and then carried her dishes inside, where she placed them on the counter beside the dishwasher. It looked like the chef and his assistant were meeting in a small nook to the side. She quickly left the room, headed out for her day. She'd be starting in the laundry room.

As she walked in, Martha stepped out. "Did you get your car?"

Forcing a bright smile, Mercy nodded. "Yes. Michael dropped me off downtown this morning."

Martha checked her watch and realized Mercy was a few minutes early. "We have a lot of work to get through today."

Mercy gave an internal cry of dismay. "The place has been scrubbed from top to bottom," she said lightly. "I'm not sure what else there is to do."

Martha gave her an unreadable look, then marched away. Mercy chose to take that as a sign nobody would explain anything to her.

She looked at her modified schedule. She had lots to do. It would be a long time before she had to ask for more work.

MICHAEL RAN ERRANDS, washed the vehicles inside and out and moved to the front yard. Never once did he go inside the garages. When he had tried, a security guard had blocked his entrance. When he explained what he wanted, the man turned to somebody else. Between the two, they brought out what Michael needed.

He walked back to the cars, figuring out how to gain access to the lower floors of the house. But that wouldn't be so easy either. This place was locked down pretty heavily.

He also didn't have any guns with him. Not that he needed them. A knife was more secretive, stealthy, more his style. By midafternoon he returned once again to yard work. As he walked to the garden shed to get the rose trimmers, he studied tracks through the fields. The estate covered ten acres, most of it cultivated landscape by the mansion. However, the other acres were hilly, and he'd never been away from the gardens. Other buildings could be here that he didn't know about.

Considering the lower levels to the mansion, it wasn't out of the realm of possibility to have outside access to those levels. But where? Once his mind went in that direction, he realized how many other options there could be. A bunker? More underground buildings? No, he would expect something within the five-thousand-square-foot mansion itself, if they were moving trucks back and forth. He hadn't seen any mansion access that could accommodate a truck, but, as he contemplated the tracks on the far side of the garden shed, he realized there was more here to see.

He put on the heavy-duty gloves for the trimmers and went back to the roses. They were thick and heavy and so in need of a trim, which could be done after the roots were well-established. He worked steadily, all the while keeping an eye on what was going on around him. He could hear noises off in the distance, past where he'd seen the tracks disappear. A road appeared to pass through the cedar hedge. But he was too far away, so he couldn't see what was going on over there.

He had seen no sign of Mercy since they had parted ways earlier this morning. He had looked for her at the little dining patio corner, but, the one time he'd walked past it, she wasn't there. As far as he was concerned, this was a stronghold, with everybody extremely well-trained. This was no place for her.

While he finished off a cluster of roses, he figured out a time frame to follow those tracks. He was pretty sure an alarm was on his room's door, probably on his windows also. He would have to disconnect those to leave and then reconnect them after he returned. He also considered a connecting door. Two apartments were above the repair garage. As far as he could tell, the other one was empty. He needed to find a way from one to the other. Absent a connecting door, he was hoping for attic access.

He finished another rosebush and tackled the one beside it. This was even bigger and older and in worse need of a trim. He returned to the shed, grabbed the wheelbarrow to collect all the rose trimmings and carried it to a large trailer used for transport to the dump, which had a special spot for compost materials.

On his return visit to clean up the last little bits and pieces, one of the security men waited for him. Michael collected
the last of the trimmings, placed them in the wheelbarrow,
laid his pruners on the top and said, "What can I do for you?"

"Take the rest of the compost to the dump now."

He nodded; he knew it made no sense as the trailer was
not even close to full yet. They were getting him out of the
way. "No problem. I was planning to do that next anyway."

"Robert is coming with you."

Chapter 10

MERCY DIDN'T HAVE time to worry about her circumstances for the rest of the day. She worked hard, kept her head down, saw nothing and heard nothing. Instead, people were friendlier than ever. She found some smiling at her and relaxing. Surely Michael was worried for nothing. Mercy worked so hard in the morning that, when lunch rolled around, she realized she'd almost missed it. She raced into the kitchen, snagged the plate waiting for her, cried, "Thanks," and walked out to the designated patio.

The weather looked like it might turn ugly soon. She hoped it stayed pleasant enough for a while so she could continue to sit outside as the seasons changed. As she sat down she froze, horrified by her long-term thoughts. She'd been getting into the role a little too much obviously. She picked up her sandwich and took a bite.

It melted in her mouth. Unlike the first couple sandwiches that were nasty and dry, this one was flavorful and packed with vegetables. She had to slow herself down from eating too fast.

Unlike earlier, when she could hear people around the corner, her noon break was peaceful and quiet. She enjoyed it. In a much happier mind-set, she went back inside. She still had one muffin in her pocket. She could save that for later. She'd eaten the other one midmorning.

She washed and rinsed her plate, setting it in the dishwasher and then turned to leave. She found the owner standing in kitchen entrance, staring at her. He didn't say anything for a long moment. She shifted her weight uncomfortably at the look in his eyes. She gave him a tentative smile. "Hello."

He nodded. "I need you to sort out some paperwork that was dumped. The pages need to be matched up again."

She brightened. She could do that. "Certainly."

He motioned for her to walk in front of him. She stepped past him and entered the big hallway. Martha stood there with a frown on her face. She glanced at the Mr. Freeman. "Right now?"

He nodded and gestured to a large room off to the side. Mercy walked in and saw a boardroom table, not quite as big or as opulent as the dining room table, with a stack of paperwork on it. She looked around for filing cabinets or something to hold the papers.

He said, "Take a seat."

She pulled out the chair and sat down.

He placed several large binders before her and said, "I'm looking for matching invoices for every one of these."

She tried not to raise an eyebrow in surprise, but opened the first binder and realized all the invoices were in order. It was a few minutes before she found the matching invoice in the stack. She held it up. "This is the matching invoice. What would you like me to do with them once found?"

He glanced at it and frowned. "Staple them together and

put them both in the same binder with a red flag affixed." He pointed to the little red sticky notes.

The invoices were signed. She nodded, stapled them, added the red flag, reinserted both matching invoices into the binder and then closed it.

She glanced at him and asked, "You want me to do that now for every one of these?"

He nodded. "Yes, and as fast as possible please."

She nodded and proceeded to work her way through the pile. When she understood which numbers the binders held, it went a lot faster. Still, it took about an hour and a half. She took note of the items, but there wasn't anything to see. Until she flipped several papers and found several handwritten notes. And phone numbers. Her breath caught in the back of her throat. She risked a glance toward Mr. Freeman. His head was down. She took another look at the numbers and committed them to memory. Then quickly returned to matching up papers. Although she checked, she found nothing else of interest.

With the finished binders laid out in front of her, she said, "Okay, I'm finished."

She turned, the smile falling off her face. He was staring at her with that reptilian gaze again. She barely held back the shudders rippling down her spine. Pinned in place, he studied her. Then with a quick nod, he shifted his gaze to the stack on the table. Sagging slightly, she stepped out of the way her breath ragged. He got up to check them, opening each, seeing all the red sticky notes, then flipping through the first binder to review each of the flagged duplicate invoices, nodded and said, "Good, thank you."

"No problem. Is there anything else?" She hoped to hell not. She wanted out of here. The information burned in her brain. She couldn't leave fast enough. She wanted to write everything down before she lost it. And then give it to someone—but who.

He shook his head absentmindedly. "Not right now, thanks."

She walked to the door and said, "Then I'll resume cleaning."

When he didn't answer, she took that to mean, yes, she should leave. She'd have to check her schedule to see what she had to do now and if she had enough time to do it. She realized she was into her normal bedding time. The bedrooms had to be set up for the guests.

She walked upstairs to the first bedroom, stripped off the bedding that probably hadn't been used ever and put fresh sheets on. As she finished making the bed, Martha walked in, took a look and nodded. "Don't forget to change the towels." Then she stopped and frowned. "Are you finished filing?"

Feeling guilty and yet not having a justifiable reason, Mercy nodded. "Yes. About ten minutes ago."

Martha gave a small smile and walked out. But wow—a smile—that was a first.

Mercy finished up the one room, put the dirty laundry into her cart and went into the second room.

So many of her actions were habit now that she walked right in, surprised to find suitcases, happy that no one was here presently. She frowned, not realizing guests were here already. She should've made sure nobody was in the room before she entered. She changed the sheets and put clean towels in the bathroom.

She knocked on the third door. When there was no answer, she pushed open the door to find this one also taken but currently empty. She quickly repeated her actions, feeling she was racing against time and not knowing why.

At the fourth and last guest room she knocked on the door. When there was no answer, she pushed it open and walked in. Somebody was sound asleep. She gasped softly catching a small glimpse of a well-known politician that was retiring and his position was going to be up for grabs. "Oh, I'm so sorry."

Her mind spun as she backed out of the room. The owner must have political aspirations. Or this man, who even now snuffled in sleep, was just a good friend. Closing the door softly, she turned to see Martha. Mercy gestured into the room and said, "The guest is still sleeping."

Martha's frown deepened as she glanced in the room. "You shouldn't have opened the door."

Mercy's jaw dropped. "I didn't know guests were staying here. I knocked, but he didn't answer, so I thought it would be empty like the others."

Martha scooted away. "I'll handle this one later. Take your laundry and get that started."

Relieved, Mercy pushed her cart down the hall to the elevator. She wasn't sure what had just happened, but Martha seemed changed. Now Martha was nervous, agitated. Was it because Mercy had walked in on the sleeping man? She hoped not. If she wasn't supposed to change the bedding, she should have been told beforehand.

Back in the laundry room, Mercy set up the new load to

wash. She glanced around, found two carts full of dry laundry to fold. She would be in the laundry room for the next hour at least.

Her mind kept going back to the scene inside the bedroom. The man had been lying on his stomach, covers up to his waist. His head was turned to the side, and his arms were under the pillows. She didn't know why he'd be sleeping at this hour, but, if he'd been up all night, it would make sense. There hadn't been anything sinister about the scene, although she was certainly sorry if she had disturbed him. She hated to think anybody who needed sleep wouldn't get it because she'd been asked to change the bedding.

By the time she finished the folding, the washing machine was ready to be emptied. She did that and straightened up the rest of the room. She still had a good twenty-five minutes until this load was dry. She walked over to the laundry basin, intent on cleaning the sink, only to find a bloody sheet soaking there. This stain had also been bleached out, turning the water pink.

Frowning, she donned her plastic gloves, realizing both bleach and some other cleanser had been added to the soak water. There wasn't a woman, outside of Martha and Mercy, here on the estate, and Mercy doubted Martha would've left her personal sheets in the sink. And Mercy couldn't imagine the guests doing their own laundry.

She gave it a good swish, pulling out the sheet enough to see the size of the bloodstain, prepared to put some stain remover on it. However, it wasn't a small stain at all. It was massive. A good two by three feet in the center of the sheet. When she realized exactly how big it was, she quickly stuffed it in the water, pulled off her gloves and escaped from the laundry room. With any luck, nobody would notice what she might've seen due to the security glitches still unfixed. Perturbed, she wasn't sure what she was supposed to do.

She walked through the kitchen, grabbed a cup of coffee and stepped out on the porch. She pulled out the muffin from her pocket and, although it was looking a little worse for wear, she unwrapped it and, sitting at the table, ate as slowly as she could.

Her mind wouldn't let it go. A huge bloodstain. She wanted to text Michael about it, but she wasn't sure where he was and wondered if she should take the chance of putting something like that in writing.

"Mercy?"

Startled, she turned to see Martha standing in the doorway. "Hi. Came to get coffee and a bite to eat."

Martha's gaze went from the coffee and muffin back to her, and her frown deepened.

With a sinking heart, Mercy realized Martha now knew about the sheet soaking in the laundry room. Even though Martha had sent Mercy there, Martha might not have connected the dots as to what Mercy could have seen.

"Did you put the laundry on?"

Mercy nodded. "I did. And I folded the two loads in the baskets. I realized the load took twenty minutes, so I came here to get a cup of coffee and a bite to eat. I'll return and grab that laundry as soon as I'm done."

Martha's gaze was assessing, but she nodded. "That would be good. Remember that you shouldn't see certain things here."

On that cryptic note, Martha walked away.

The longer Mercy thought about the sleeping man and the bloody sheet, the more worried it made her.

She finished her muffin and coffee, stood, cleaned up her place and walked back to the laundry room. As soon as she entered, she knew the sheet would be gone.

The smell of bleach hung heavy in the air. The other washing machine was running, and the dryer had stopped. She didn't dare check the washing machine to see if it contained the bloody sheet.

She knew the sink would've been cleaned out perfectly. If any security cameras were working in here, they had already seen her checking out the sheet earlier.

At the dryer, she pulled out the bedding she'd taken off earlier and quickly folded all the sheets. With everything stacked for Martha to put away, Mercy stopped for a moment, rubbed her face and wondered how long she could keep up the pace. She had to remind herself that she had promised Michael to only stay today.

By morning she'd leave for sure. The trouble was, things were getting interesting. And way more dangerous.

ROBERT HAD BEEN hovering for hours. The trip out to the compost dump was delayed as Michael found several more rosebushes to deal with. He still couldn't figure out why he had the bodyguard for an escort. But it made Michael highly suspicious of every movement on the estate.

He walked to the garden shed, replaced all his tools and made his way again to the trailer. He dumped the rest of the load of his clippings, returned the wheelbarrow to its storage spot and walked to one of the utility trucks they used on the property. He grabbed the keys, hopped in and backed up to the trailer. He quickly hooked it up, knowing Robert stood close by, watching to see how Michael did. It would be a long, cold day before they saw him mess up something so simple. He'd been driving trucks with trailers for over a decade now. He quickly connected the lights for the back of the trailer, walked around to the driver's side and climbed in again.

At the gates, in a half-joking manner, Michael said, "Make sure you don't lock the gates behind me. I want to get back in again."

The man lifted his face, but he never said a word.

Keeping up the pretense, Michael gave a friendly wave and drove onto the driveway to the main gates. As he pulled through, he caught sight of Mercy standing in front of the big windows. Once again she was cleaning. He glanced at Robert sitting beside him and said, "How come you're with me?"

Robert shrugged. "Orders."

Quietly Michael nodded. He wondered what the order was about exactly. To watch and to make sure Michael didn't go astray? That would be easy enough. At least on the surface. But he had an investigation underway. "Settle in for a drive. It takes about fifteen minutes if the traffic is light to get there."

Robert never said a word.

Michael strummed his fingers on the steering wheel and then fiddled with the radio. "You don't mind music, do you?" The cab filled with a country twang.

Robert looked at him and groaned.

Michael gave him a bright smile. "I love cowboys."

Robert shook his head and stared out the window.

At the dump site, Michael quickly backed up to the designated pile, grabbed his gloves off the dashboard and got out. Before he closed the door, he motioned to a second pair gloves. "If you want to finish faster, feel free to grab the gloves and give me a hand."

Robert gave a snort.

Michael laughed. "Yeah, I didn't think so." Whistling, he closed the truck door, hopped into the trailer and tossed out rosebush cuttings. Realizing the truck window at the back of the cab was open and calculating Robert's position, Michael instinctively chose a spot to work where he wouldn't be an easy shot. Besides the constant awareness of everything, he couldn't get rid of the idea that Robert had plans to drive the truck and trailer back himself—minus Michael.

As soon as he was done, he pulled a broom from the truck bed and swept out the trailer. As Michael and Mercy were finding out, this place was nuts for cleanliness.

He kept watching to see if Robert made a move in any way. The whole time Robert appeared to be sleeping. Mystified, Michael opened the door, got back inside, and started up the engine. "Taking a beauty nap?"

Robert nodded. "I need to catch five anytime I can."

Michael filed that away for the future. Were all the security men short on sleep? And didn't think that would change anytime soon? That's the only thing Robert said all the way back to the estate.

When Michael was inside the gates, he reversed the trailer into its usual position. He looked at Robert and said, "Guard duty over?"

Robert shot him a look. "What are you doing next?"

Michael studied him for a long moment, then looked at the grounds, wondering what he'd done to deserve a bodyguard all day. "I'll probably weed the back garden." He glanced at the sky as he hopped from the truck. "The dead heat of the day is gone, and it looks like rain tonight, so this would be a good time to get some of that weeding done."

"If you say so."

Michael laughed. "It's a great way to spend the afternoon."

And no matter what he did, Robert was right there. Never talking, never helping, but always there.

With Robert so close, Michael couldn't study the layouts, couldn't watch any of the other activities, couldn't make his way to the garage, couldn't do anything. When he walked back a couple times, Robert stopped him. He got the message—stay in the gardens; don't return to the house or the garages.

Finally he glanced down at his watch. "Four o' clock."

Robert snickered. "What? You think you're on salary? That you have start and stop times?"

Michael planted his hands on his hips. "Yeah, I do. I started at eight. I plan to do a little bit more, but I'll be quitting soon."

Robert looked him up and down for a long moment, then nodded. "What are your plans after that?"

Michael shrugged. "No definite plans. See if I can find somebody to have dinner with me—or not."

"You using one of those new dating hookup apps?"

"Not likely."

"Maybe you should. Women are a dime a dozen on there." Robert smacked his phone in his pocket. "I can line a dozen up anytime."

"I haven't checked out the apps yet."

Robert walked Michael to his apartment door. "It would be a good night to get the hell out and stay out for a while." He gave him a hard glance and said, "Get my meaning?"

"Loud and clear. Any objection if I ask the maid to go?"

Robert's gaze wandered over to the maid's quarters and back again. "No, that might be a good idea. Curfew is still 10:00 p.m., or you can't get back in until the a.m." With that, he left. But he didn't go far. He only went over to the vehicles, where he had positioned himself to watch whether Michael went into his apartment or not.

Rather than doing more work, Michael pulled the keys from his pocket, unlocked his door and walked in. He carefully locked the door behind him. Moving quietly he checked out his space to see if anybody had been here. As far as he could tell, no one had.

He set about putting on coffee, his mind spinning. His thoughts were to get out for a few hours and still be back by ten. But he didn't like how they'd stepped up security. Something was going down tonight. He needed to be here to find out what the hell it was. At the same time, he wanted Mercy a long way away. He sent her a quick text.

Dinner?

If she was still working, would she take the chance of answering her phone? The response came back a few minutes later.

Sure. I'm done for the day. I was told to go to my room early. I'm off to take a shower.

Text me when you're out.

Will do.

He smiled. He hoped she got dressed and packed up at the same time. Because, when they left, no way in hell would he let her come back.

While he waited, he headed to the bedroom. In the large double closet on the right side was an attic door. There were boards against the short wall hammered in place that he could climb.

Bingo.

He lifted the small square of wood off to the side, he climbed up and took a look around. The attic was empty and had no solid floor. But, by walking the rafters, he moved a few feet forward and grinned.

Exactly as he'd hoped. A second attic door.

Just to be sure, he silently removed the second hatch and peered below. A dark closet. He slipped to the floor and opened the closet door enough to see the room. It appeared empty, and the bed wasn't made for company. Taking a chance, he did a quick tour of the apartment to reassure himself no one was here, then moved back to the closet. It was harder to climb up from the floor, but he managed.

Back in his own place, he waited for Mercy to text him that she was ready. In his head though, he was making plans ...

Chapter 11

S TEPPING FROM THE shower, Mercy dressed quickly. She didn't have much in the way of changes of clothes, but she put on a clean pair of jeans and a T-shirt. She'd had a decent day, although a hardworking day. She knew Michael would fight her about staying another night, but she wanted to. And, once she told Michael about the bloody sheet and a guest sleeping during the day, he'd understand too. These were some worrisome events, and they might find more clues related to the deaths of Sammy and Anna.

Speaking of which, she texted the detective as promised. Then turned her attention to her personal belongings. Not that she had many ...

Deliberately Mercy left the last of her possessions packed in her bag and on the bed. Ready to grab if in a hurry. She didn't want anybody to see her walking out with the bag on the off chance they were watching her. But she certainly was not one for hauling all her clothing around. With any luck she should be back tonight with no problems.

She locked her door behind her, went downstairs and outside. It was about six o'clock. She walked across to Michael's apartment and knocked on his door. No answer. She frowned. She had said she would be here in a few minutes. She couldn't imagine he'd go anywhere in the meantime. She stepped back and looked up toward his window and knocked a second time. Still no answer.

One of the security men came around the corner. He stopped when he saw her and frowned.

Hurriedly she asked, "Is Michael around?"

He shrugged. "The last I saw, he was over by the vehicles."

She brightened. "Okay. That makes sense." She quickly passed him, heading for the driveway and garage. She didn't see Michael out front, neither did she see his truck anywhere close by. She pulled her phone from her purse and texted him.

Where are you?

There was no response. Disturbed, she spun around in a slow circle, looking for him. He had to be somewhere. He wouldn't have left without her.

Feeling that horrible sense of unease coming back again, she turned to find a different security man. "I'm looking for Michael."

He nodded and smiled. "He said he might ask you out for dinner tonight."

She smiled. "Yes, he invited me, but I can't find him."

"He's been doing errands all day, so he should be around."

She glanced at Michael's apartment. "I knocked, but he's not there."

He retreated a few steps, his hand on his hips.

She frowned and walked away. "I'll try again. He's probably in the shower." Turning, she confirmed nobody was watching her this time. She raced back to his apartment. She pounded on the door hard. Still no answer, so she tried the doorknob and pushed it open. It wasn't locked. She raced upstairs to another door. She pounded on that one too. When she didn't get an answer, she tried the doorknob, but it was locked. So he was either locked inside, or someone had walked up behind him and ... Under her breath she muttered, "Shit."

She pulled out her phone and called him. It rang and rang.

Getting really worried now, she slowly made her way back downstairs, figuring out her options. Maybe ten minutes has passed. But obviously he'd either been sent somewhere or had taken an opportunity to find out something. Of course a more horrible sensation that something had happened to him wouldn't let her go. She didn't want to take her thoughts down that path. It was tough enough as it was. The last thing she wanted was to be constantly worried about where he was. Then again he said that's how he felt about her.

She sat on the stairs between the two doors and waited. After a few more minutes she picked up the phone and called again. Still no answer. As she hung up, a text came through. It was from Michael. With relief she read his question,

Where are you?

Outside your apartment.

Be there in two.

She stayed put, hoping he meant it. When the bottom door opened, she jumped to her feet and raced to meet him. It was a sign of how nervous she'd been when she threw her arms around him and gave him a hug. "I was so worried about you. I texted you multiple times, phoned you several times, and nobody seemed to know anything."

"I had to go on another errand. It took a little bit longer than I thought."

She nodded. "I thought, when you asked me about dinner, you were off duty."

He shrugged. "I was, but I am supposed to do what I'm told."

She glanced around nervously and asked, "Can we leave now?"

He wrapped an arm around her shoulders, leading her to the side of the building. "We'll take my truck and head into town."

They passed several security men. She called out cheerfully, "I found him."

No one said a word; they just watched as the couple walked past. He helped her into the passenger side of his truck, walked around it and got in. He turned on the engine, and, in silence, they drove through the gates.

She started to speak, but he held up a finger to his lips as if to silence her. He hit the button on the small remote in his pocket and did a quick sweep of the cab with his arm. When there was no sound, she asked, "What are you doing?"

"Sweeping the truck for bugs."

He turned the machine off, dropped it beside him and said, "It's all clear."

She sank back in the seat. "I can't believe you think like that all the time. How could you do this job as a career?"

"I *used* to do this. I'm out now. Except for this special

case."

She glanced at him. "I'm sure there's more to the story than that."

He shook his head. "Not really. I did a number of years in the US Navy. After an injury, I stepped out and didn't return. The last year I have been ranching, generally doing physical jobs a long way from anybody."

"Right. I guess that makes sense."

"I'm only back in action because of Sammy's disappearance."

"You mean, his murder," she corrected him softly. "Yeah, while I understand your reason for doing this, this is the only time I've ever done anything like this."

He pulled onto the main road and headed into town.

She relaxed, opened the window slightly and said, "How did your day go?"

It sounded like a stupid old-married-couple question, but, given the situation, she'd love to know if he found out anything.

"Busy. I was given a bodyguard early on, and he stuck with me the entire day."

She gasped. "Really? Why? Do they know what you are doing?"

He shook his head. "I don't think so, but I presume something is going on that they didn't want me to accidentally see. Every time I went to the garage today, I was stopped. When I headed out in the back, behind a certain section of the garden, I was also stopped."

"That sounds very suspicious."

He shrugged. "Who's to say? For all I know, they're

blending a new form of wine from the estate's vineyards and didn't want anyone to know the special formula." His lips quirked in her direction. "Or there may be bodies they don't want anyone to see."

She shivered. "It's nothing to joke about."

He sobered. "Sorry, I've always used humor to deal with the dark issues in my life."

"And that's the way it should be," she said quietly. "It's hard for me to remember that my sister was one of those dead bodies."

That killed the conversation until they reached town. "Where are we going?" she asked.

"To a nice little Italian restaurant around the corner."

She nodded. "That sounds lovely. I have something I need to tell you. I guess I'm a little scared. Maybe I'll tell you inside."

He nodded. "Good enough."

He pulled into a parking lot and hopped out, took off his jacket and laid it on the seat then opened the passenger door for her. Together they walked into the restaurant and were given a table under a beautiful stained-glass lamp in the back.

Once settled, she watched him gauge the other customers before he leaned forward. "What did you see?"

The waitress walked over then. They ordered coffee as she delivered menus. When she disappeared again, Mercy leaned forward. "I was in the laundry today after changing the beds. Oh, that reminds me ..." She stopped for a moment and shook her head. "So there are two things. First I was told to change all four guest bedrooms. I did three, realized belongings were in two of them, so there were guests at the estate that I didn't know about. At the fourth door, I knocked and opened it up when there was no answer. A man was sleeping on his stomach, his head turned to the side, and the bedding down at his waist. He's a local politician I think. I backed out of the room and came up against Martha, who was really angry that I went in."

"That's understandable. We don't want to disturb the guests, now do we?" he said in a sarcastic tone.

She nodded. "Then I went to the laundry room with all the bedding I had switched out, starting one load, folding others. When I had put it all away, I went to the sink and found it was full of bloody water."

Now she had his interest. She glanced around the restaurant to make sure nobody could hear and added, "A sheet was soaking in there with a very large bloodstain in the center, at least two by three feet. However, the water had a heavy bleach smell and several other chemicals you spray on for stain removal. So I imagine, whatever it had been, it was thoroughly degraded as far as a forensic analysis goes," she said. "I left soon afterward and went to get some coffee. Martha came into the kitchen. She seemed angry I'd been at the laundry but kept it in control. When I went back to pull out the rest of laundry from the washer and the dryer, the sink was completely empty but the bleach smell was strong." She leaned closer. "And she warned me about not seeing things that weren't my business."

He settled back and studied her. In a low voice he said, "Then maybe my joke about dead bodies wasn't far off."

She nodded, taking a sip of her coffee. As she set down the cup, she said, "That's what I was thinking of when you said it."

"Was the man alive or dead that you saw *sleeping*?"

She winced. "I heard him and he moved slightly, so I'm presuming he was alive and well. There was no sign of blood."

He nodded. "Good enough."

She bit her lip as she stared at him. "But now I can't get that thought out of my mind."

"Sorry. That question had to be asked."

"Shit," she groaned and stared around the restaurant. "I never even had a chance to check. I walked in, ready to change the bedding, saw him and quickly left."

"What about the other people in the other rooms?"

She shrugged. "The bedding had been pulled back as if someone had just gotten out of bed. One had a suitcase on the bed as if they'd pulled some clothing from it."

"And all the rooms had male guests?"

"I didn't see much, but the bag in the one room looked masculine. The clothes were men's too."

"Well, don't worry about it for now. I haven't seen any cars, although a lot of extra security is around, so I'm not sure, but maybe some of the people staying in the house are part of his security detail."

Her face brightened. "That would make sense, wouldn't it?"

"Only if you've got something special planned, or he's particularly worried about something."

She nodded.

Then the waitress returned, asking if they were ready to order.

They looked at each other and down at the menus they

hadn't even opened and shook their heads. As the waitress left to give them another few minutes Mercy opened the menu and saw the dinner special.

"The special looks good," Michael said to Mercy.

She nodded, closed her menu and said, "Order two of the same. I can't say I care at the moment."

AFTER THE WAITRESS took their orders and left, she came back with baskets of fresh warm sourdough bread and butter. He watched as Mercy's eyes lit up. He nudged the basket toward her and said, "Give it a try. I've been here before and love the bread." So saying, he grabbed two pieces to put on his plate. She was fast to follow. "Has the food improved at the estate?"

She nodded, not bothering to speak with her mouth full. When she finally swallowed, she said, "Today was much better. Plus, I got a couple muffins for my breaks."

"Good. I was afraid you wouldn't get any decent food today."

She shook her head. "For some reason, they decided to feed me well."

He snorted. "The Last Supper does come to mind."

She shot him a look and then sneaked another piece of bread. *How could he convince her to stay away tonight and never return to the estate?* He wanted to explore without having to worry about her.

He turned his head as the front door opened, then back to her. In a low voice, he said, "Don't look now."

She froze, her gaze locked on his face. "Why not?"

Casually he glanced around the room as security men he'd seen on the estate passed. "Two of the men from the estate came in."

She tilted her head to the side as if contemplating. "They could be just enjoying dinner?" she hazarded a guess.

He shook his head. "I highly doubt it. Security has been pretty darn tight all day." He settled back in the chair and smiled at her, enjoying the way she licked her lips, like a cat that had just had a special treat. She was cleaning up the little smidgen of butter at the corner of her mouth. "Maybe they are still with me. Maybe they decided they couldn't see anything from the parking lot and better come into the restaurant themselves."

She frowned at him, reached across and patted his hand. "That's okay. I'll protect you," she said in a cheerful voice.

He gave a half snort. "Really?"

She gave him an innocent baby-blue look and shrugged. "Nope, sorry. I'm pretty useless when it comes to self-defense."

The waitress returned with heaping plates of food and quickly left them alone. Mercy's eyes lit up at her dinner.

He was glad he had brought her here. After a few days on the estate where she hadn't had enough food and had worked so hard, her body was in a constant state of hunger. "Maybe they're worried about you."

She grabbed the pepper grinder and proceeded to add pepper to her plate. Michael watched the waitress who talked with the security men. She took their orders and disappeared into the kitchen. "Well, they are staying to eat," he muttered. "Of course that made their cover more solid."

"It must be pretty irritating when you had one of them on your butt all day, but it could be an innocent visit."

He raised his head and shot her a hard look. "Do you really believe that?"

Instantly the cheerful look on her face fell. After a moment she shook her head. "No, obviously I don't. I was enjoying the fantasy of the moment."

He felt like a heel. "And I'm sorry for blowing that. I don't want you to get so wrapped up in the fact that you believe they're good guys."

"I also can't get wrapped up in the fact they're all bad guys either. They can't all be guilty. For all I know, there is just one bad rogue among them."

He didn't bother answering. How could he? She didn't know Sammy like he did. There was no way one guy could sneak up behind Sammy and take him out. Not like that. For all he knew, her sister had been involved in everything and then shot as a traitor. But this surely wasn't the time and place to question her sister's guilt.

Brusquely he said, "Don't return."

Chapter 12

MERCY APPRECIATED WHEN the conversation switched from work to something much different. She really liked Michael. That he was here to protect her, to find answers for his friend, endeared her all the more to him. That this was what he had done as a job and was willing to step back into for his friend was even better. She loved a man who wouldn't take no for an answer when it came to helping a friend.

It'd been a long time since her last relationship. The breakup had been painful, and she hadn't been willing to jump back into the arena. There were so many dating apps now, but she wasn't interested and had removed them all from her phone. Even though her friends constantly asked her about her latest date, she'd been happy to just shake her head and say, "Hell no."

Not one of them knew anything about where she was right now. If they thought she was having dinner with Michael, they'd be all over her, wondering what app she had found him on. The thing was, it wasn't an app; it was real life. She wasn't a fan of the new dating trend. At the same time, she knew the difficulties in meeting people locally. Still, she had met Michael accidentally. So, if she wanted to indulge in a fantasy right now, to think it was a date, just the two of them in a safe, secure little world, what harm would that do? That two security men from the estate who were at the same restaurant didn't have to be all bad either. If she hadn't ever heard about her sister and Sammy's murders, she might wonder if the two security guards were best buddies, or maybe they were a gay couple, and this was their one and only chance to get out.

Immediately her mind glommed onto all these scenarios and went over a half dozen more. Maybe they were meeting because they planned to open up their own cupcake shop. She could feel herself grinning foolishly. And yet, it felt so great to add some humor to the moment. There'd been so much tension and strife and hard work these last few days. It felt good to laugh at something.

"What's the smile for?"

She wasn't sure if she should share or not but shrugged and explained.

His eyes widened. "Gay? Cupcake shop? What, like a butcher shop?"

She laughed, loving the fact he hadn't mocked her for her fantasies. "That's such a male macho thing," she said. "You guys do eat more than just your fill."

He pointed to his plate. "Hey, that's not fair. Look what I'm eating now."

She nodded. "Probably the one time in at least a couple weeks you had seafood and pasta. Am I right?"

He chuckled. "In this instance, you are right, and that's only because my meals here have been somewhat limited. Lots of nights I just had sandwiches at my apartment."

"I wondered why you didn't come in with the rest of us in

the house."

"It's my choice," he said. "Although I don't think they want me inside. I also don't see the security guards eating in the house either."

She shook her head. "I don't think I've seen any of the security men eat inside either."

"You don't see many of the men in the house. Exactly what goes on in there?"

"That was the other thing I needed to tell you." She glanced around the room to make sure she couldn't be overheard. "Today I helped with matching up invoices in all these binders and on the back of one of the pages I saw several numbers," she said then spilled out the phone numbers she'd memorized. "I was so afraid he'd see me."

"Did he?" Michael asked sharply. "Because if so you're out of there tonight."

Remembering the look in Mr. Freeman's eyes made her shudder all over again. "He was looking at me strangely. But he does that a lot." She winced. "I'm always looking behind me feeling like I'm being watched."

"And I really want you out of there." He had his phone. "I'm sending those phone numbers to the detective and Levi. They should be able to find out who's on the other end. Although that's a good lead, it's damn dangerous in that house."

She shook her head and smiled. "No. It's okay. He's always like that. But after helping him, I was, of course, behind in my cleaning"—she rolled her eyes—"and that's when Martha sent me to change the beds for the four guest bedrooms." She groaned.

"The owner is quite a famous figure around here I'm sure he has many high powered friends, yet it would be good to keep track of any that are close. But the bloody sheet is …"

She watched him struggle for the right word. "It's worrisome but I don't know that it was terrible." She shrugged. "Besides the owner is the kind of person I won't remember after I leave—except for the fact we have some suspicions. Otherwise, he's fairly …" She struggled to come up with the word, then added, "Ordinary."

"Most people would *not* say that." He sent another text message. She figured he was filling them in on the phone numbers.

She forced her mind back to Mr. Freeman and away from the possibility of another murder. "When he's talking to his peers, he's probably got a powerful presence. Whenever I see him, he's not really talking directly at me, so no power is in that smile nor is his charisma turned my way. Therefore, he passes through my life as yet another male." She shrugged. "Although, when I first crossed paths with him, I thought something was almost reptilian about him. But he was different today."

Michael frowned. "Interesting."

She dug into the seafood, loving the soft succulent shrimp. "This is delicious." She glanced up. "I'm surprised you're not having a drink."

Surprise lit his eyes. "Would you like one? A glass of wine perhaps?"

She shook her head. "No, it puts me to sleep. Are you planning on going out later?"

He turned that stormy blue-gray gaze her way and raised

an eyebrow. "I'm planning to take you wherever you need to go, then going home to sleep," he said in a neutral tone.

She snorted. "Like hell you are."

She watched as he slowly put down his fork, propped up his hands and rested his chin on one palm. "I wish you'd stay away, but you won't."

"And I wish you would stay in your room tonight, but you won't either."

He frowned at her. "I have to find out what's going on."

She nodded. "So do I."

He picked up his fork and took another bite, slowly contemplating her expression.

"Remember I promised I'd leave no later than tomorrow morning, not tonight."

He nodded. "What will you do if you run into trouble tonight?"

"I'll run to your place." She grinned, then chuckled. "If you are who you say you are, then you shouldn't have any trouble protecting me."

He shook his head. "It doesn't work that way. Protecting you when you're in my apartment is one thing. Protecting you when I have no idea where you are or what you are doing is a completely different thing. And, if you end up running to me, and I'm not there, then what?"

He had a valid point. She had always thought, if anything happened, she would run to him. But what if he wasn't there? What if he was out, doing a little sleuthing of his own? If she was being followed, she could wreck his plans too. In fact, she could put them both in grave danger. That wasn't what she had wanted.

"Then I guess I'll have to run for the woods," she said quietly. "I wouldn't want them to come looking for me at your place, only to have them find out you're not there." She watched as he turned his gaze from the two security guys sitting at the far side of the room.

"There is no place on the property you would be able to run to and be safe," he said quietly. "I wish you wouldn't return tonight."

She didn't know why she was still arguing with him about this. Part of her didn't want to return ever again. Part of her knew she had to. She hated that. "I feel like I need to be there."

He put his fork down a little too forcefully and glared at her. He opened his mouth, thought better of it, and lifted his coffee.

After he took a sip, she placed her hand on his. "I'm not trying to be difficult."

"But you are," he bit off. "This isn't a game. You should take what happened to your sister as a warning."

She squeezed his fingers and let her hand fall away.

As they were about to break contact, he placed his hand over hers. "I don't want anything to happen to you."

"It won't. I promise."

He shook his head. "Your promise wouldn't necessarily change anything. These people are not playing games."

Then the waitress asked, "Is there anything else I can get for you?"

Michael smiled up at her. "No. We're good, thank you."

The waitress looked from one to the other, then backed away. As she left, she detoured over to the two security men.

She stopped and spoke with them, her gaze going to Michael and Mercy's table, then back to the two men.

Michael's fingers clenched convulsively around her hand. "I don't like that development."

"And yet, she's serving them too, so it would be instinctive to go from one table to the other."

"It doesn't matter. We need to get the hell out of here, and we need to slip by them."

"How can we leave here without them noticing?" Mercy asked. "We have to walk right past them to get out the front door."

"Which is exactly why they're sitting at that table." Michael surveyed the room as she watched him.

"Is there a back door?"

"There is, but we don't need to use it." Michael glanced at her plate. "Finish up. Then we'll leave."

She nodded and quickly ate the last few bites on her plate. As she watched, he pulled out cash from his wallet and tucked it under his plate. It was a generous amount, more than enough to cover their meal and the tip. He pulled out his phone, sent a text, then put it away again.

She nudged her plate slightly out of the way and said with a happy smile, "Regardless, I enjoyed that."

He smiled at her. "Good. Happy to hear that. I'm glad you accepted my invitation."

"It's not a real date," she said in a teasing way.

There was a warm look in his eyes. "Oh, it's a real date."

She rolled her eyes at him but loved to think he meant it. "Thank you for dinner."

He inclined his head. "You're welcome. Maybe next time

we'll find a place where we can stay a little longer."

She grinned. "I'd like that."

He pushed his plate away, picked up his coffee cup and said, "In a few minutes there will be a disturbance. I'll get up, grab your hand and disappear out the front door in a way they won't see us. You understand me?"

She took a sip of her coffee and coughed. She cleared her throat, nodded and reached for the water glass. "Thanks for the warning."

He outstretched his hand; she placed hers in it. "Are you ready?"

She studied his features, then nodded. "Sure. I don't quite understand why or how, but I trust you."

This time when he smiled, it was breathtakingly intimate. "Thank you. That's what this is all about."

Then the door opened, and a large group of people came in and milled around the front of the restaurant as if looking for seating to accommodate them. They crowded around the table where the two security men sat. And that's when Mercy understood. Instantly, his fingers closed over hers. She was out of the chair, led to the far side of the restaurant, where he quickly swooped her past the large group. Luckily they had parked on the opposite side of the building so didn't have to cross in front of the security men again.

He helped her into the truck, walked around, fired it up and, without turning on the lights, pulled away. As soon as they hit the main road, he turned on the lights and kept going. "Now where can I drop you?"

"You have to return tonight. I have to get my car."

He shot her a hard look. "I could easily pick the car up for you."

She shook her head. "No. By the way, that was a neat trick. Obviously you have a lot of people in your life you can call on in moments like that."

"I have good friends I can count on, and that's worth everything."

Then headlights shone in the back window. "Shit. It's them."

NOW HE HAD limited options. Taking her back was likely the safest thing at this point. He had little other choices—other than to pull over and have it out right now, and that he couldn't do without blowing his cover or getting her mixed up in the middle.

"It'll be way too obvious if we pull over to the side of the road and let them pass." He glanced at her, a hard look still on his face. "It's not safe for you."

She twisted in her seat and stared at the vehicle behind them. "Okay, I think I'm finally convinced you're right." She turned to look at him. "But what are we supposed to do now?" She realized he was slowing down and approaching the estate. "I don't know how dangerous this is, but, if you stop here, we may be able to run away into the surrounding countryside."

He shook his head. "Not possible. They also have security cameras outside the estate."

"Are we thinking my life is in danger?" She glanced around at their tail. "It's too surreal to believe I go out for dinner and come back to get shot."

"When you've packed up your things, then you can come over and spend the night at my place."

Startled, she gave him a small cry. "Why?"

"Because at least that way I'll know you're safe. I won't get a wink of sleep if I don't know that."

"I thought you would go out and search the property."

"And I still might. But I need to know you're stashed somewhere safe."

"I doubt your place could be considered safe," she said with a half laugh. "It's obvious we're coming back here together."

The gate opened wide for them; the security guard waved.

As Michael drove past, she said, "On the surface they all look so welcoming."

"Of course." He watched in the rearview mirror as a second vehicle drove in. Everybody waved back at each other. He wondered if he was making too much of it. But he sure as hell wished he'd gotten her away first. Why the hell had she been so resistant?

"Drive over to the big house. I'll head up to my room. You return to your place, and then I'll sneak over."

"Chances are you won't be allowed to," he said. "Remember the intruder who stands outside your door?"

She nodded. "I might be able to get out. If not, you can come and unlock my door."

He gave a snort at that. "They could be up to something else. I don't know what it is. It's cameras and bugs I'm worried about now." He pulled up to the servants' door.

She grabbed her purse, gave him a bright smile, and hopped out. She closed the door, walked over to the back entrance, and opened the door to the staircase leading to her room.

When she was safely inside, he pulled the vehicle over to his side. He parked it, ready to go should he need to. He unlocked the entryway door to his apartment and headed upstairs, his mind churning. He needed one more good night where he could go outside and check around. But what he needed to do first was get her the hell out.

A text on his phone caught him unawares. He pulled out his phone to see it was from Levi.

Any news?

Something's going down. Suspected third death. Suspected artillery stockpile. Looking to find a holding place on the property. Saw new tracks to back of property.

Guns?

I'll tell you in a couple hours.

And the girl?

Still stubborn. Still here. But not for much longer.

He walked upstairs, unlocked his apartment door, checking to make sure all was well as he answered Levi. Be nice to have a phone call with him later tonight, but Michael didn't dare risk it. Just because he'd searched for bugs didn't mean he had to do it all over again right now. He put on a pot of coffee and took the opportunity to sweep the rooms. That there were no bugs made him even more suspicious. It worried him they had something more sophisticated. Like monitors. In which case, they would already know who he was because they would've seen him searching for bugs. He turned on the TV to give himself a bit of cover noise and walked into his bedroom to change into a black shirt. He shut off the lights in the living room and left the light on in his bedroom. It was too early for him to go to bed, but it wasn't unexpected to think he might be sitting up in bed, on his laptop, before going to sleep.

He checked his watch. It was now ten-twenty. There was no sign of Mercy. He walked to the living room window, keeping to the side of the glass, with the curtains for cover, and checked her room. He was in time to watch her lights go out.

He stood silent and watched the grounds around the estate. Every once in a while, he watched one of the security men on the perimeter route as he checked out the property. Mentally Michael noted the time. He waited until he watched the man come back again. No, it was a different one this time and thirty minutes later. In those thirty minutes there was no sign of Mercy. He wondered at her choice to stay here. Or was she waiting for the right time when it was safe? He'd wait several hours before it was clear for him to go out.

As much as he liked the idea of having Mercy stay at his place, he also didn't like the idea that somebody might come here to search, finding her. It would be okay if that person found the two of them. But if they found only her, then they'd know he was checking things out. They'd also believe she was involved.

He stood here, sipping his second cup of coffee, watching as a small figure slipped from the stairwell and walked across the yard toward his room. He hadn't seen the security guard standing outside her room tonight; that was a bit of a concern too. No need for the routine to change unless something bigger called the security guard away. And anything that changed the routine made him cautious.

He opened the door downstairs before she had a chance to knock. He quickly ushered her inside and closed the door behind her. Motioning for her to go ahead, they climbed the stairs to his apartment.

Upstairs she glanced around. "It's nice. Much bigger than my place," she said in surprise. "You have a kitchen too."

He nodded. "I haven't done much cooking yet."

While she wandered through his place, he walked to the window, watching. Placing a finger to his lips, he went to his bedroom and did a full-on search to see if there was anything suspicious. He found a tiny camera on the other side of the bed. Angry, he stared at it, wanting to rip the thing off and toss it down the toilet. Instead, he knew he needed to use it. He sat down on the bed out of view for this camera and pointed at it.

Mercy frowned but kept quiet. She walked close to him and, in a surprise move, wrapped her arms around him and gave him a kiss. Up against his ear, she whispered, "Then we should use this."

He wrapped his arms around her waist and held her close. She was right, but he didn't want to put her in any more danger than she was in now. And, inside himself, he could feel his loins stir. It'd been a year since he'd had a relationship, a year where he'd shut down that part of himself fully and tried to heal so many other aspects of his psyche. But now, with this warm, willing, gorgeous woman in his arms, it was hard to think of anything else. When she plastered herself tighter against him, reached around his neck, her lips against his, he realized she really meant it.

Chapter 13

MERCY COULD FEEL his shock and surprise when she wrapped her arms around his neck and pressed so close against him. She wasn't in marketing for nothing. She knew exactly what needed to happen. It was all about creating the intended impression. Right now people needed to believe the whole reason she was here was to make love with Michael. That they'd be busy for hours.

With her lips close to his ear, she whispered, "Let me lead."

But his hands were too busy stroking up and down her back, and she wasn't sure if he got the message she wanted him to get. It was hard to keep her head as passion flared between them. What was supposed to be a marketing exercise was quickly spiraling out of control. She hadn't expected to melt at his touch—to want to jump his bones and assuage the need clawing at her. But then again, who could've imagined something like this? He was igniting a response inside her that she hadn't felt in a long time. Maybe in forever.

Perhaps it was the taboo of being watched. And maybe it was just this incredibly sexy male who had his hands all over her, sending her hormones into overdrive. Whatever it was, the feeling was incredibly delicious. But she had to keep her head. She tried to keep her mind and body separated, but he was doing his best to seduce her, and her body was a willing partner.

She hoped he got the message, because, in a few minutes, it would be a hell of a rude awakening when she pulled back. She wasn't trying to be a tease, but they had the window that they needed. When he had urged her back against the bed, her legs coming up against the mattress, she shuddered. She gave a shake of her head, trying to clear her mind, pushing the raging heat down before she lost all sense of what she was doing. She slipped out of his arms, her breath ragged, her breathing hoarse in her chest. And standing in front of the camera, she pulled her T-shirt up and over her head. And tossed it right over the lens.

With a shaky breath she paced the room, trying to calm down. When he grabbed her shoulder, he leaned forward and whispered in her ear, "Remember it's an audio and video device."

She rolled her eyes, knowing what he meant. And threw her arms around his neck and kissed him hard. He picked her up, carried her to the bed and together were now fully focused on putting on a show to create a sweaty session of sex in audio alone.

When he finally rolled off her, she clapped a hand over her mouth, stilling the giggles. He looked at her and grinned. She rolled her eyes again and pulled the covers to her mouth to stifle any sounds. He stood and walked quietly into the other room. She lay on the bed for a long moment and let her breathing relax until she calmed down to the pretense of falling asleep. Rolling over, she slipped to her feet and tiptoed out. They had to leave the door open and the lights off.

In the other room she found him with a cup of coffee in hand, standing by the window, looking out into the night. His breathing had calmed—better than hers had—and she knew he was contemplating his options. She slipped up behind him and whispered, "Do you think it's safe to leave?"

He reached an arm around her and pulled her against his chest. After what they'd gone through, it felt so natural to wrap her arms around him and hold him close.

"I'll give it a few minutes. Let them think we've gone to sleep."

She rubbed her cheek against his bare chest.

He squeezed her gently.

"Is it wrong I wish that wasn't for show?" she whispered, needing him to know she cared. He was going into a dangerous situation. She wanted him to know he wasn't alone.

He stilled and crushed her tighter against his chest. His heartbeat picked up and raced against her ear. He leaned down and whispered, "We can pick that up again later."

She chuckled and in a throaty whisper said, "In your dreams. Not with video and audio." His chest against her skin made her smile deepened.

"Not sure I want to leave you here alone," he admitted against her ear.

"Considering they think I'm sleeping off a hot sweaty sex session, I don't think you need to be worried about me."

"Maybe, but I did find a way that I think will keep you safe in case they do come." With his finger against his lips, he led her to the hall closet outside the bedroom. On the ceiling was access to the attic. A couple boards nailed against the wall acted as a ladder for accessing the space. He pushed the lid up and out of the frame, and she popped her head in and over. There was a handle to secure the attic access in place again. She made her way back down and looked at him. "Is it normal to have something like that?"

He shrugged. "It's normal enough. If they had trouble with ventilation, or if they had to add fiberglass for insulation or any other number of issues, it would make sense to have attic access. What it does do is give you a hidey-hole, in case you hear anyone coming. It also connects to the other apartment so you can escape that way."

Back in the kitchen she realized somehow he had gotten changed and was completely dressed in black. He looked like a cat burglar. When she said as much, he gave her a slanted glance and asked, "How do you know I'm not?"

She raised an eyebrow, thought about it, and smiled. "No, your morals and ethics are too high."

This time his eyebrows shot up. "How do you figure that?" he asked curiously.

"Because you're all about keeping me safe. You're all about finding out the truth about your friend. And you're all about putting the bad guys away. If you were a burglar, you wouldn't care about all those things."

He studied her intently for a long moment and then smiled. "Stay safe," he instructed as he walked to the bedroom where the attic door was, then he looked back at her.

She shoved her fingers into her jeans pocket as his gaze slowly lowered to her breasts, swollen and plump in her lacy black bra. She glanced down and blushed.

"As far as images to take with me," he said in a gravelly

voice, his gaze hot, "this is the best."

HAVING THAT LAST image of her tucked away safely in the corner of his mind, Michael slipped out of the second small apartment and down the stairs. He checked for alarms but didn't find any. Soundlessly he opened the outside door and stepped into the night and into the hedges at the side. He waited for his eyes to adjust. As soon as he could see clearly, he set a course toward the large garage. It ran along the wall right to the back of the property and then connected to the hedge. That would give him a clear path into the back corner of the property. There was no sign of anyone as he made his way across the short but exposed grassy area. At the garage he pressed his ear against the door, but no sounds came from inside. Going up to a window, he looked inside, but it appeared dark and empty.

Crouching below the window, he carried on to the back of the building. From here he connected to the hedge, and within seconds he ran softly down the path to a good hundred yards of cedars. Lots of places for him to blend in with the darkness. The moon cut in and out of the clouds above, giving him enough light to see his next few steps, only to yank away the visual within seconds. Good thing he had great night vision.

He was pretty sure the bad guys must have another space here. He was partial to the idea of an underground bunker. The trick was getting there without being seen. Casting an assessing gaze, he quickly decided the cedar hedge offered the most protection. When he made it to the hillside and crept down the slope on the far side, he'd been out just under fifteen minutes. He hit the stopwatch to record the time.

At the bottom of the hill he could see where the gravel road beside the cedars ended. Not one vehicle was in sight. From here, he couldn't determine if a door or some other structure was around the corner of the hill. He waited, his ear tuned for noises out of the ordinary. Something small rustled in the underbrush next to him. Most of the animals would be sound asleep by now. The only ones out at this time were the ones hunting. Just like he was.

When he heard nothing further, he picked his path carefully across the rocky ground. He moved from boulder to boulder, silent in the night. In the distance he thought he heard something. He crouched low to the ground and waited. When the noise didn't repeat, he skulked forward yet again. The gravel road dipped, and, as he followed, he could see a truck parked against the hillside. It appeared to be empty, but he couldn't take that chance.

After several moments passed with no one approaching the truck, he raced up behind the truck and crouched at the back end. The pickup had a canopy over the top. He peered into the windows but didn't see anyone. There wasn't any reason to have a truck down here, unless it was being used for something.

The keys were still in the ignition, and a rifle rack was inside the truck, but it was empty. He quickly took a picture of the inside of the cab, crept to the front to get a snapshot of the license plate. He sent both to Levi and the commander.

Hidden behind the pickup he studied what appeared to be a manmade cave in the hillside. What could have started as a cave had been reinforced with timbers and maybe steel. It looked like a big warehouse. He assumed some kind of enclosure kept the wildlife out. But, at the moment, it was open.

What were the odds there were no lights? If people were inside, there should be lights inside. He studied the dark opening with suspicion. Had they seen him coming? He debated waiting until he had some assistance but knew the next time he came, whatever this place was, would be locked up tight.

Trusting his instincts that said to get in there and find out, he stepped across the threshold and went around the first corner. No alarms went off, at least none he could hear. They spent a lot of money building this place and would need to spend a whole lot more if they wanted to set up security on something so large. He certainly would have if it'd been his place. But this looked to be in the middle of construction. And considering how well it was hidden, security might not be a priority for them.

Tucked up in his hiding spot, he let his gaze slowly wander, waiting for yet another layer of darkness to settle in. With his eyes adjusted, he could see crates on one side and tables on another. An open space in the center had tracks in the middle of the dirt. He couldn't imagine what anything this big would be used for. It could easily hold a couple 18-wheelers, even concealing the emptied trucks and their unloaded cargo. The pickup truck sitting outside wouldn't carry much weight compared to what had driven in here.

He studied the turnaround space outside. It was awkward, but any good driver could back a vehicle in and out. Sticking to the shadows as he moved to where the stacks of crates sat, he could see at least six. They were locked down. He desperately wanted to turn on his cell phone flashlight. He didn't dare take the chance. With his ears tuned to the slightest noises, he lifted the lids off some of the crates. As he bent to the front of one and tried to force it open, he could hear voices. He slipped behind the crate, realizing he was up against a stone wall. He hunkered down and waited as the voices came closer.

"We need to get these out of here tonight."

"We can't move up the timetable that fast," a man argued. "No need to panic. Early in the morning we'll get the second shipment. They could both go out at the same time."

"That's more dangerous. Better that they go out one at a time. If one gets picked up, the other will still be safe."

"This isn't a fly-by-night operation. We've been planning this for months and months now."

"And yet, there have been problems," said a man, his voice cool. "Robert had to take out four different people."

"They were all connected. They shouldn't have been involved in the first place, but we were very short-staffed." He snorted. "And it's not fair to include the maid and her spy boyfriend. They should have been taken out early on."

"We had to wait until we had proof of their snooping," a second man said. "And now that that's been taken care of, are we expecting any more trouble?"

"Not now. We have this morning's work to clean up still and without my political friend who is also here finding out," the man with the cool voice said. "That driver should never have been killed in bed while he slept. Especially not when the bedroom beside his was fully occupied. Not to mention we needed information from the driver first. Had he acted alone when he stole a crate? Or did he have help? This was badly done."

"Not to mention, you have people working on the estate who have nothing to do with this, and, if they find out …"

"Then the same thing will happen to them that happened to the others," said the second man angrily. "We have a lot of people working in this place now. Only a few are involved. We intend to keep it that way. But we still need people to help when things go wrong."

"That's the way we want to keep it. Profits can only be divided so far before there is no profit left."

"What about the supplier?" The man with the cool voice spoke again.

There was something almost familiar about that voice, but Michael couldn't place it.

"He hasn't gotten back to me."

"Well, maybe you should deal with that and not worry about the logistics here."

"It's all connected. I don't intend to lose out on any of this."

"None of us do."

Michael listened to a bit more of the wrangling until the three men stepped up to where he could see their shadows. They kept walking, past the crates, and out into the night. Michael quickly retreated until he was at the corner, staring at their backs as they stood beside the truck. He caught one picture but knew he'd only see outlines, maybe their profiles if he was lucky. One of the men walked around the truck and hopped into the driver's seat, turning on the engine. The other two men got into the vehicle. The truck turned around expertly and left.

When he thought he was in the clear, he heard a weird rumbling and a steel door came down almost in front of him. He had a split second to decide if he would stay inside or out. He chose inside. With a sense of foreboding, he watched as the heavy steel door clanked to the ground and sealed shut—locking him inside. He turned to the rest of the room and said, "Well, shit."

Chapter 14

H OW LONG WOULD Michael be? Mercy never thought to ask him before he left. And she should have. Because every damn moment seemed like an hour. He'd only been gone half an hour, but it seemed like half the night had passed already. It was painful to sit here and wait for him. She knew he was fully capable of handling whatever came his way, but nobody could outrun bullets, not even him. He might be a specialist in his area, but how many bad guys could he realistically take on? One person in hand-to-hand combat, sure. What if they had knives? Her mind set up many scary scenarios. All of them with Michael ending up severely injured or worse—dead.

She kept think of something else, happier, more cheerful, and then her mind glommed onto her sister and Sammy's murders. There was nothing cheerful in her life at the moment.

"Not quite true," she whispered to herself. Because having Michael in her life was a huge boost. Not only was he helping her on her quest to get answers but he was doing his utmost to keep her safe at the same time. Knowing he was part of her life made her feel so much more confident about what they were doing. He was one of those can-do type men. One of the ones who walked into a room and asked what needed to be done and buckled in and did it without sitting there discussing it. She loved that about him. That he moved with the effortless grace of a panther added to his appeal. Which, if she admitted to herself, was a damn sexy package.

Since his hands had done plenty of wandering around her body, she knew he was definitely interested in her. There'd been no way to fake the ridge against her pelvis when they'd been in that tight clench. Or any way to mistake her own electric response. Even now, she wished they were in bed together, making good on the promise they'd made.

Her experience about those things was more limited. Maybe because of her sister who'd been such a wild child, sleeping with every teenage boy she could get her hands on. Because of that, Mercy had held back and was much pickier about her choice of lovers. Remembering the feel of Michael's arms and hands on her body made her go hot and flush all over. He'd be a hell of a lover. There was something about that passion—that heat was like being enveloped in the scorching trail of desire. Something she'd never experienced before.

She enjoyed sex, loved the cuddling afterward, but she hadn't had anyone open up the passion inside her—a hunger that she'd felt only with Michael. It had been all she could do to pull back and not get caught up in the moment of their fake sex scene. She'd do a lot for another chance. But it wouldn't happen while they were here. Remembering that others might still be listening, she tiptoed back into the bedroom, quietly stretched out on the bed, rolled over and made heavy sighs as if she was waking and falling back under again. Then she lay there, dry-eyed, staring at the ceiling with worry.

How much trouble could he get into on the estate? What if he came upon something illegal? What if the security men caught him skulking around? Was that what had happened to her sister? There was no way to know. And that bothered her.

To hold down this job like Anna had meant to keep it, she'd straightened up and knew how to put in a full day's work. If she'd had similar work over the years, this might not have seemed so hard to her. Maybe because she'd had to work. Maybe the work load hadn't been quite so bad for her.

Mercy had no clue how Sammy fit into this. But she was happy her sister had found him. That she hadn't been alone at the end. It also made Mercy feel better to know Anna hadn't been involved in anything illegal as she'd been with Sammy, who Michael had assured Mercy had been the opposite of a bad guy.

She rolled over and stared at the doorway, hating these ever-so-slowly lengthening moments. Michael should have returned by now. She headed for the bathroom. Back on the side of the bed, she checked her watch again. One hour. He'd been gone only one hour. She closed her eyes and tried to sleep. Not that she had much hope of it. She listened for any sound—both good or unnerving.

She didn't dare miss anything. Especially not if there was any chance somebody would come here looking for him. Although if they did, she didn't have any way to keep them out or to let Michael know he was in trouble.

As she lay worrying, she thought she heard a voice outside. She slipped off the bed, walked over to the bedroom window. His apartment was on top of the garage. There were windows on both sides. Hidden from view behind the curtain, she studied the dark evening outside. She could see nothing. But she hadn't mistaken the voices. With her ears straining, she stayed still and waited.

That's when she saw the men approaching the downstairs door.

MICHAEL QUICKLY CHECKED along the seal of the huge door, looking for a way out. With the vehicle outside gone, he took his cell phone out of his pocket and turned on the flashlight. He'd take the chance using the light with the men gone. His gaze followed his fingers as he ran them up and down each side of the heavy metal door. There had to be a control mechanism for those on the inside. It would be foolhardy to seal people in and not have a way to get back out. Although …

He glanced around, deeper into the large space, realizing a way out could be in the back as well. Swearing at himself for getting into this situation and yet intrigued by everything here, he was conflicted. He shouldn't have left Mercy alone for so long. She would be worried. And yet, this was what he came to find.

He walked to the crates, knowing if he opened one and they saw any sign of that, they would know somebody had been here. He was hoping to find one already open or at least with some lettering on the side. He checked them over, but all were sealed.

He took pictures of what little he found and sent them

out, only to realize he had no signal. Swearing, he moved through the space, looking for other items of interest. A lot of mechanical parts were stacked up, with empty pallets off to the side. Beside those was a stack of small crates.

He stopped when he saw the writing on the side. *C-4.* Was that how they were creating the space in here? Surely not. It would take some pretty skilled dynamiting to create the space without blowing the top off the hill. He frowned as he considered the cave.

He kept going deeper and deeper, past the pickup trucks until he hit the far wall. He was afraid of burning his cell phone battery out using the flashlight the whole time, but this was a necessary process. In the back he was confronted with another door frame under construction. It looked like they were still expanding backward, and this was the last of the support beams. Nothing was stored this far back.

Moving swiftly he crossed to the far side. There were workbenches, tables, desks and a couple trailers. It looked like they were setting up for some big production but weren't to that point yet. Dismantled shelving sat on the floor ready to be assembled.

There was a space where the digging and framework was going in, but they hadn't put a door in. The cave wall was still solid as no opening had been created yet.

And so Michael was sealed in. But not for long.

Back where he'd started, he ran his hands up and down the space around the big steel door. He didn't know of one single door that didn't have a control panel on the inside. Remote control on the outside made sense, but a keypad control panel should be on the inside regardless.

He found a set of wires connected to a series of controls. They hadn't been mounted to a control panel yet. Still he could work with this. Moments later, he heard the steel door creak and groan as it slowly raised itself. The problem with this was, if he opened it, once again they'd know. If he could open it a few inches aboveground, it would be enough for him to get out, and, if he found a way to jam it back down again, no one would know he'd been here.

He played with the door for a good ten minutes, finding a space that would work for what he needed. Several empty pallets were on the side. Knocking them over, he set the door to stop at that height as if the mechanism was blocked. When he got it down, he dropped all the wires, raced over, and, on his stomach, he squeezed under the doorframe. Free and clear, he brushed off and raced back the way he'd come.

As he finally approached the hedge, he wondered if Mercy was okay. It looked like the sentries were walking the perimeter yet again. They did that once an hour, and he'd left soon afterward. He still had open ground to cross to get to the main garage the guards had worked so hard to keep him out of. He waited for the men to continue past him, slipped up to the main garage and waited, satisfied he'd made it without being seen, but still surprised to find the guard detail gone from here. Maybe because of the 10:00 p.m. curfew? He peered into the closest window.

No sounds came from inside. He tested the door. It was locked. He pulled out his tools and quickly picked the lock. He let himself in and closed the door behind him with a soft *click*.

Once again he stood in place and listened, letting his eyes

grow accustomed to the darkness. Two large trucks were here—similar to the ones down in the cave. He looked in back to see what they were carrying.

Wooden crates. To gain access wouldn't be easy, as they were all strapped up. Taking a chance, he turned on his cell phone's flashlight to see if there was any lettering. Again nothing. He quickly shut it off, moved to the second truck and found the same thing. For whatever reason, these two heavily laden vehicles were stored here, and nobody was allowed access. Money? Drugs? Weapons? He had no idea but suspected with everything they knew so far, it was going to be the latter. But all of the above were bad news.

As he walked to the side, he caught sight of two men coming around the corner outside the window. Instantly he ducked down, out of sight. They walked past him, heading to the old garage. Shit. He didn't dare let them get into the apartment and find her alone. He raced back to the entrance of the other apartment, opened it, and crept up the stairs.

Inside, he climbed into the attic and crossed to the hatch into his apartment.

Mercy stood beside the window, studying what was going on outside.

In a low voice he hissed. She spun in shock and saw him.

Relief washed over her face, and she threw herself into his arms. He held her close and whispered against her ear, "Two men approaching my door."

She nodded frantically. "I saw them. They tried the door earlier, but it was locked. Then they left."

He nodded. "I presume they are back with the keys."

He dragged her toward the bedroom. With quick fingers

he stripped down and motioned at the bed. She understood and stripped off her jeans. She crept in under the covers. He pulled her up against him and held her tight.

Within minutes they heard men on the stairs. There was no knock on his door, but he heard a key inserted in the lock, and his apartment door was opened into the living room.

Anger flushed through him. He sat up and called out in a snarling voice, "Who's there?"

He bolted from his bed, threw on his jeans and raced out to the living room. His angry gaze landed on the security men with his fists clenched. He slowly let out his hot breath and demanded, "What the hell are you two doing in my place?"

The two men looked at each other and back at him. "We didn't think you were here."

He raised an eyebrow. "Where did you expect me to be? Are you searching my apartment? What the hell?"

The two men backed up a step. He took a step forward.

"Are you alone?" one of the men asked in a hard voice.

He snorted. "What the fuck business is it of yours?"

They stopped for an answer. He understood their quandary. They'd come expecting him not to be here for whatever reason. Had he been seen? Then he heard movement behind him.

Mercy stuck her head around the door; then she stepped out, wrapped up in the sheet. In a low whisper she said, "I'm here with him."

The men relaxed. They nodded and smiled at her gently. "Sorry for disturbing you." They shot him a look and then retreated.

He called behind them, "Lock the door behind you, and

lose the key."

They didn't say a word; they just shut the door.

They deliberately didn't relock it. He walked over, locked the door, grabbed a kitchen chair, and propped it against the doorknob. He turned back to her and said, "Nice timing." And grinned.

Chapter 15

MERCY STARED AT Michael, in shock at his words. "*Nice timing?*" she whispered. She shook her head and continued in a barely audible voice, "It doesn't matter. That was way too damn close. And now we're in deep shit too."

The smile fell from his face. "Are you going to be fired, do you think?"

She thought about it, rubbing her temple. "I don't know," she said. "I didn't see a No Fraternizing among Employees sign." She shrugged. "I'm sure Martha will have a rule against it though." Mercy frowned, her mind working the angles. "You think that's why my sister was killed? Because she started a relationship with Sammy?"

He walked over and gently wrapped his arms around her, tucking her close against his chest. "I hope not. I would doubt she'd die for something so simple."

She winced. "I keep wracking my brain, wondering if she would get involved in something shady like this. The trouble is, I can't answer that question. When she left, I would have definitely said, 'Yes.' She was into drugs, men, and the fast life. She probably stole, shoplifted—hell, I wouldn't be surprised if she wasn't involved in some shooting or breaking and entering back then. But we didn't hear from her for a long time, and she grew up somewhere along the line. To think she was here for several months cleaning like I've been cleaning"—she shook her head—"it boggles the mind. She never would've been caught doing menial labor before."

She pulled back from Michael's embrace, hating that lassitude overcoming her, wanting to stay nestled close to him. "What about the rest of the night? Do you think I should return to my place?"

He shook his head. "Hell no."

She frowned. "I left my toiletry bag in the bathroom."

"Is it that important?" he added quietly, "It's past 10:00 p.m. curfew."

The two stared at each other as if across an impasse. Then she shook her head. "It's not, but I don't want to leave anything of me behind. I know that doesn't sound right, but it feels right to say it. There is something so very wrong about this place that I want to make sure I take away everything that's me." He raised an eyebrow at that, but he didn't mock her, for which she was grateful.

"In the morning I'll walk over with you, and we'll get it."

"And what is your excuse?"

"I wasn't planning on using an excuse," he said. "If I have a lady stay for the night, I always make sure she gets home safe."

She frowned at him.

He raised a hand when she went to argue and said, "No arguments. We need sleep."

"Ha, like I could sleep now." She walked back into the bedroom, the sheet falling slightly. When she'd dashed from the bed, she'd pulled the straps of her bra off her shoulders.

She quickly pulled them back up. In her panties and bra, she tossed the sheet back on the bed and remade it. "We've already destroyed your bed tonight."

"So no reason we can't destroy it again, is there?" he asked with a devilish note in his voice.

She shot him a smirk. "You should be so lucky."

He pointed to her shirt, still over the camera.

She nodded.

He quickly divested himself of his jeans while she watched, her heart speeding up at the bulge in his underwear. She deliberately closed her eyes and pulled the blankets up against her shoulders. Because the truth was, she did want to roll over and welcome him into her arms and rip up the sheets. But that was hardly the best idea right now.

And she'd never want an audience.

She lay there pondering the ins and outs of relationships as he got into bed behind her. She held her breath as the bed swayed as it took his weight. Finally, she rolled over and whispered, "I don't think the bed can take any more shenanigans as it is."

He gave her a startled look, then a shocked laugh. "I'm not that heavy," he whispered in protest.

She chuckled but hopped out and stood, looking at the bed frame. She motioned him out of the bed. "Get up and help me lift this mattress," she murmured.

Obediently he got out of bed and checked out the footboard and underneath the mattress frame. *Cracked*, he mouthed.

He held up a finger and then pointed at an odd crack in the frame. He bent over the footboard. She scrambled around the side of the mattress where she could take a look. Something was jammed in there. Michael pulled out his tools.

"It must be from the way you sat down," she whispered, her tone flirty.

Michael muttered, "Like hell."

She grinned, but her eyes were sharp as she watched him pull out dog tags.

Pain whispered across his face.

She knew instinctively they were Sammy's dog tags. And there was nothing she could do to help him through this moment.

He dug in again with his tools for anything else, and, sure enough, a slim USB key fell out.

He snagged it and put it with the dog tags, checked to make sure the little hiding space was completely empty, then as quietly as possible, they replaced the mattress and remade the bed. When they were back in bed, he plugged in the USB to his laptop and took a good look at what Sammy had stored there.

Photos.

Photos of the cave that Michael had been in tonight and of the men unloading crates of weapons and crates of C-4 explosives. A man stood off to the side, holding a semiautomatic machine gun, dressed in jeans and a black T-shirt. The second photo was of Freeman, the owner of the estate, standing beside one of the open trucks and speaking to somebody else Michael didn't recognize. It looked like packets of money were handed over, but the photo was too far away to make that distinction. He studied the photo.

She squeezed his hand, knowing Michael was also dealing

with the loss of his friend.

With a smoldering look in his eyes, he leaned over and kissed her. But not just a kiss of *Hey, how are you?* or a kiss of *Hey, we'll get through this.* This was a kiss of *Holy shit, I can't wait to hold you in my arms and devastate your self-control.* Most definitely it was a promise. For later. The trouble was, she wanted that promise now. She didn't want to wait.

What if something happened to her, like to her sister? Life was too damn short for waiting until she knew somebody better. What a fraud she was. She wanted this man any way she could get him. But what she didn't want was to have him while somebody else was listening in. Decision made, she slipped from the covers and walked to the living room.

She checked the time. It was almost three in the morning. She walked over to the teakettle, filling it with water slowly, soundlessly. She would have to catch it before it whistled too. In the dark she stared at the moonlight outside. A bone-chill settled in. She couldn't forget the people who had been in this same position and hadn't survived.

He'd followed her out of the bedroom with his computer and closed the bedroom door almost to the point of latching it. He sat down at the kitchen table and opened the other folders found on the USB key. Waiting for it to load seemed to take forever. "I knew Sammy would leave something useful," Michael said quietly.

Finally the file opened, and she could see literally dozens of folders. She walked over to make tea for both of them. With two cups in her hands, she returned to the table, sitting beside him, her heart seizing at the very first image. It was her sister. A happier, contented sister. Anna, in Sammy's arms, stared at the camera at the end of his arm as Sammy took a selfie of the two of them.

"Oh, my God," she whispered. "I never thought to have recent pictures of her."

Michael wrapped an arm around Mercy's shoulders and urged her closer. She moved the chair until they were touching, and she snuggled up against him. She brushed away the tears as she looked at the sister she hadn't seen in twelve years.

"She looks so happy. So very different from who she had been when she left home," Mercy murmured.

"It happens that way sometimes," Michael said as they continued their whispered conversation. "Think about it back then. She was probably having trouble fitting in, looking for something other than the life you and your mom represented. She went wild, had to find herself, figure out what she was doing. But it looks like she did it eventually."

"And Sammy? How does he look?" She studied the man in the photo, his face revealing a strength of character.

"He looks like he adored your sister," Michael said.

"It's so damn unfair." Mercy shook her head. "How could somebody kill those two people? They had their whole lives in front of them. They had finally found each other and looked like they could be going somewhere."

Michael nodded, his chin rubbing against the top of her head. "Sammy was a good guy. He would've been good for Anna."

"And she would've been good for him. Help him live a little."

They flipped through several of the photos, more selfies— the two of them in town, on the estate, and in this very apartment. "I wonder how long they were together?" Michael asked.

"I have no idea," she whispered. "I tried asking questions about her, but no one was willing to talk to me."

"Most people probably don't know the details. And those who do won't be talking."

"Of course not."

There were a couple pictures of Anna alone. And then several of Sammy alone. Each time was a different location. Michael and Mercy studied the backgrounds for any purpose as to the location. But, so far, they weren't coming up with anything. Then she froze. "Is that the cedar hedge?"

He leaned forward and nodded. "And that one is further down." He tapped another one. "In the background is the storage warehouse I found."

Excited they ran through the photos in that file, they went to the next folder. This one held photos of the estate and every one of the security men, all still employed here. A list of their names and notes on each security guard were also in that folder.

"Why would he do that?" Mercy asked.

"Standard procedure. So everybody knows who the players in a scenario are. Just in case …"

She felt sick to her stomach when she realized Sammy had documented his own murder case, fully aware he could become a victim. She shook her head, tears in her eyes once again. "Poor Sammy. Poor Anna."

Michael wrapped his arms around Mercy and squeezed her shoulders. "Yes, now it's up to us to make sure they didn't die in vain. We have to stop these assholes. So they can't do this again."

THE LAST THING Michael wanted to do was sleep. He had a beautiful woman in his arms, one who had very quickly captured his heart. She was so damn loyal that he couldn't help but admire her. She was also full of surprises. Like when she'd pulled off her shirt and tossed it over the camera so he had the chance to head out and search the grounds. She also saved him once again when she came out of the bedroom, wrapped up in the sheet. Looking delightful. The woman was prepared to do what needed to be done.

She slowly disengaged from his hold to cradle her head in her arms atop the table.

He was worried about her. She jumped first and looked second. She was so concerned about her sister's life and her sister's death, but Mercy would have to walk away, leaving the investigation to the professionals. And he knew she had no intention of doing that.

The only thing he could do to help keep her safe was to get answers for her. Answers for the both of them. She wouldn't like that. She was on the stubborn side. He smiled, realizing he liked stubborn.

"Stop thinking so hard. You're keeping me awake."

Her sleepy murmur had startled him.

She had her head resting on her forearms on the table. He chuckled. "Go to sleep so you can't hear me thinking."

"I would if I could, but that's not possible," she whispered.

"Try again." He gently stroked her arms up and down in a

soothing, comforting motion. She still had her bra and panties on. "You sure you want to keep your bra on? You can't be very comfortable. Are you chilled? Do you want to get changed? Your clothes are here."

"I'm fine. I figured it was safer to keep this much on."

He raised an eyebrow at that. "Safer?"

"You're a little too sexy. I figured any barrier, even a tiny thin one, would help," she said with a smirk.

He lowered his head and dropped a kiss on the curve of her neck. "And you're too damn sexy even with it on." He stood and walked to the couch. He took off the cushions and pulled out a bed, much to her delight. He scooped her up and laid her on it.

She rolled over slightly and raised her heavy eyelids to stare up at him with leashed passion in her gaze. Her lips quirked in a sexy gesture at the same time.

That pulled at his heartstrings. He lowered his head and kissed her on her cheek, then on the tip of her nose. "Go to sleep," he whispered.

"Sleep is looking further and further away from my mind," she murmured.

"That's not good," Michael said, trailing kisses down her jawline. "You need rest."

She slid her arms up around his neck, tugged him closer and whispered, "Maybe we'll sleep a little bit later." And she kissed him. Unlike his kisses, hers were not teasing or slow and relaxed.

Her heat, her need, met his heat and his need, made his temperature soar. He wrapped his arms around her, holding her full length, pressing his hips against hers.

She curled more fully and settled into his pelvis, gently pressing harder against him. He heard her take a deep breath.

"Well, lady, you don't fool around."

She chuckled. "So what exactly is this then?" she teased.

He flashed her a grin. "This is serious business." He lowered his head and unleashed the passion inside.

It was all he could do to control himself as her hands slid, stroked, encircled him, her tongue sliding delicately over his sensitized skin. Her hot kisses pressed against his neck and with a fervor he recognized—because it matched his.

She kissed him again and again and again with a heat that quickly overtook him. He pressed her into the mattress, their bodies hot, demanding, needy. When she opened her legs and wrapped her thighs tight around his hips, he groaned and pulled back, lowering his head to rest against the curve of her neck as he took several deep breaths.

"I need you," she whispered. "Now."

He shook his head "I don't want it over so fast."

She tilted his chin up so she could look him in the eye. "Next time we'll take it slower."

He bit off an oath when she slid a hand down and circled him, then squeezed. There was no holding back no matter how much restraint he might want to have. Within seconds her panties were ripped off and his boxers joined them on the floor.

With the last bit of his control, he rolled to his side and gently slid a hand between her legs. He found her hot, wet, and more than ready for him. She cried out as he probed delicate skin folds, spreading the moisture on her outer lips. She twisted beneath him, trying to pull him on top of her.

Finally, she grabbed his ears and tugged him down, kissing him with a hot, ravishing openmouthed kiss.

With a groan deep in the back of his throat, he moved on top of her and settled into place. She wrapped her arms and legs around him like a monkey, pulling him deep inside her. He froze there for a long moment, then, with a feral cry, moved. There was nothing relaxed or controlled about any of his movements. It was a wild, frantic coupling, as if an elastic band stretched too far had suddenly snapped.

Suddenly she clenched him tight, cried out, and climaxed in his arms. He plunged deeper—once, twice, three times—before he exploded. Exhausted, he propped himself on his elbow for a long moment, then eased his weight to the side while still staying within her. He dropped his head to the pillow, desperately trying to control his breathing.

When he could, he lay beside her, Mercy wrapped up in his arms. Into the silence of the night he whispered, "Do you think you can sleep now?"

But there was no answer. He listened to her steady breathing and grinned.

Apparently she could sleep just fine.

Chapter 16

WAKING TO FIND herself in Michael's arms was a unique experience. Even in sleep he cradled her protectively. His body was wrapped around hers to keep her safe. From the circle of his arms she smiled at the world, wondering how she'd gotten so lucky. Mercy had never expected to find somebody here. Obviously, she hadn't gone looking. But she hadn't had anybody in her life in a long time. And that made finding him that much more special.

Everything had changed with him, and she didn't want to lose him. It was time to get out. She knew she'd promised him that she'd leave this morning, yet she'd been looking for a way to change his mind. But now, waking up with him, she realized how precious life was all over again. Making love with Michael had reawakened and affirmed that she wanted to pursue her life as well as to honor her sister's.

It was odd how she'd known this truth before, but the reality hadn't been brought home to her. Not like it was now. She snuggled deeper into his arms and enjoyed the moment.

Daylight came through the window, so it was definitely morning. As she didn't plan to go to work, it probably didn't matter what time it was. But she didn't want any confrontation if she could avoid it. She also had to get her belongings and her car.

She struggled to reach for her phone on the side table without waking Michael. As she came up against his arms, they tightened around her and tugged her back against his chest.

"It can't be morning already," he murmured.

She twisted slightly, stretched up and kissed him gently on the lips. "It is morning. I just don't know how late."

His eyes popped open, and he stared down, a warm welcoming smile in his eyes. He leaned over, effectively locking her underneath him and gave her a hot good morning kiss. Then he bounded up off the bed, leaving her panting for more.

She shook her head. "You can't do that and walk away, you know?"

His grin was mischievous as he grabbed his phone.

She studied his nude body, loving the play of muscles and bone on a perfectly fit, healthy male in his prime. "He really is beautiful."

He gave her a startled look, and she realized she'd spoken out loud.

She flushed slightly, then shrugged. "Why hide the truth? You're gorgeous."

He shook his head and checked his phone. "It's just after six."

"And that means time to get up."

He opened his laptop, checked for emails and then checked his phone for messages. He shook his head and then whispered, "Nothing from anyone." His voice was resigned.

She understood the feeling. They wanted answers. They

wanted action. They wanted something right now. And it wasn't to be.

He walked into the kitchen to put on coffee. She rose and headed to the shower. As much as she wanted to drag him in with her, there was no time. Nothing like the light of day to remind her of the danger they were both in. Especially Michael, after the security guards came into his apartment last night, unannounced. But would he leave with her?

Mercy knew the answer. No way in hell. Inasmuch as she admired that, she also hated it. Back in the bedroom she dressed quickly.

In the kitchen, she found Michael already dressed, and he had poured two cups of coffee. He handed her one and whispered, "I should go after your toiletry bag alone."

She looked at him in surprise. "Why?"

"There's no foot traffic outside. Given the hour, there should be people moving around."

She shook her head. "I don't understand. What difference does that make?"

"*Change.* Something's off."

She walked to one window and studied the immediate surroundings of the estate. He was right in that she couldn't see anyone walking or driving around. She walked to the other window. Then shrugged. "It is early."

"No, not here." His voice was hard, meaning no argument.

She decided it really wasn't an issue. "Fine. It's on the counter."

He gave her a big grin. "Good. That's what I like to hear." He threw back the rest of his coffee and said, "Back in five."

He disappeared out the apartment door and down the stairs.

She watched from the window as he went to her room. The door to the house was locked. *Interesting.* He did something, and, within a minute, he was inside. She couldn't see him as he went in but saw his shadow at the top of the stairs. Her room should've been locked as well, but he took care of that in seconds. Apparently, he was a very adept cat burglar.

She watched him walk into the bathroom, then come out with her bag in hand.

A few minutes later, he stopped at the window and stared at her directly. She gave a half wave; he tilted his head in acknowledgment and stepped from her room. She saw his shadow briefly, and then he disappeared from sight.

When he was at the bottom door, she watched two men approach. "Shit. Now what?"

MICHAEL WAS ABOUT to step outside when he thought he heard voices. He quickly stepped back behind the closed door and waited. Sure enough, he *had* heard voices.

"Who checked the security this morning?" one of the men asked.

"That was Steve's first check. What do you want to bet he botched that job too?"

One of the men grunted. "He still has a job. If he'd screwed up, he wouldn't be here now."

"He only has a job because we got trouble right now and need every hand on deck."

The door was pushed wide open, and the men walked upstairs, busy wrangling over staff problems. When they were halfway up, Michael slipped out of the door before it fully closed. Knowing time was very tight, he ran the distance, sprinting through his door and back upstairs.

"Come on. Let's go," he said as soon as he saw her.

"Don't I need to talk to Martha and tell her I quit official-ly?"

He shook his head. "No time. Let's go. Now," he finished sharply.

She nodded and beat it down the stairs. They went the other direction, coming up on the far side of the garage. He walked to his truck, disarmed the alarm, and opened the door for her. She jumped in and sat down.

As he walked to the driver's door, his name was called. He turned round, watching one of the security guys walking over to talk to him.

"Where you going?"

The man's voice held curiosity, but he didn't appear aggressive in any way. And, as such, Michael answered honestly. "Taking the new maid into town. She quit this morning."

The man snorted. "That's no surprise." He glanced down at his watch. "When do you start?"

"Not until 7:30."

"What about her car?"

Michael shrugged. "She's pretty overwrought at the moment. I'll make arrangements to take it to her later."

The henchman nodded. "Get going and be back in time for work."

"Yeah. I haven't even had breakfast yet," Michael said with a smirk. "I'll grab something at the drive-through and be back."

The man grinned. "You know that stuff will kill you."

Michael laughed and called back, "All kinds of things in life will kill me." He opened the truck door, shoved the key into the engine, turned it on, and headed out. He glanced at Mercy, slouched in her seat. As he approached the gates, they opened up for him. He drove through without hesitation.

Chapter 17

A S SOON AS they went through the gates, Mercy straightened up and looked around. "We made it out?" She
hated she said it with such surprise. Of course they made it;
Michael had seen to it. She shuddered. She had no idea if
anybody was after her yet, but it felt like they'd made it clear.

"Absolutely. They don't have any reason to suspect you of
anything."

"Maybe not but it won't take them long to add two and
two together."

He shrugged. "Better that you are nowhere near this when
it blows up."

She couldn't agree more. Except one thing bothered her.
"I need my car."

He nodded. "But first you need to be a long way from
here."

"Easy for you to say. I have my real job to return to. I
need to head home, do some laundry and get my life back on
track, but I need my car for that."

"That's fine, but, as you still have time off coming to you,
I would like you to spend a few days with a friend of mine—
to make sure, when this goes down, they can't go after you."

"What?" She turned toward him, startled. "I don't want

to go anywhere but home."

He pulled into a coffee shop in town and said, "That might be what you *want* to do, but what you *need* to do is to stay safe." Michael parked the truck at the side of the coffee shop. "You must understand how it may not be safe at your place."

She shook her head. "I don't want to hear that."

He opened her door and led her inside the coffee shop.

They walked to a table, and Michael said, "When this is over, you can return to your place."

The waitress approached and asked, "Can I get you anything? A menu and coffee?"

Michael nodded and smiled. "Yes, please."

Mercy dropped into her chair and glared at him. "Fine. Get me coffee. It won't make a damn bit of difference."

"Eating breakfast won't make a whole lot of difference either," he said, his voice hard.

The door opened to the restaurant, and a man and woman walked in. Mercy couldn't help looking up when the door jingled. Michael glanced at the incoming pair and nodded. The woman was strikingly beautiful. They approached their table and sat down beside them, surprising Mercy. Instinctively she moved over to make room.

The beautiful blonde looked at Mercy and said, "Good morning. I'm Ice."

Mercy smiled. "That's a very unusual name."

Ice nodded. "But then Mercy is not very common either."

She raised her eyebrows. "You know who I am?" She glanced at the man Ice had walked in with, who had similar features in that he was a tall blond, with that same can-do attitude. Obviously these two were a couple.

"Do you guys work with Michael?"

"No, but we're hoping Michael will work for us," the man said with a smile.

She glanced at Michael. "I didn't know you were changing jobs."

"Not changing my job. When this estate business is over, they want me to go into the business with them."

She turned toward the other man who held out his hand.

"I'm Levi."

She shook his hand. "Michael's very good at his job."

Ice chuckled. "That he is. That's why we want him to work for us."

Mercy turned to Michael. "Why won't you?"

He gave her a flat stare.

She forged on regardless. "It would be good for you. You won't feel so rootless."

He leaned forward, his eyebrows shooting up. "How the hell do you know that's how I was feeling?"

"You had no problem dropping everything to look after Sammy, did you?" she asked in a reasonable tone. "Whatever it was you were doing, you weren't enjoying it as much as this kind of work."

He sat back and gave her a narrow look.

She grinned. "And you thought I didn't notice things."

After that, the conversation turned to more general issues and never once on the mess at the estate. She presumed it was too public a place for that discussion.

After breakfast, she stood and excused herself to go to the washroom. She figured Michael would ensure she left with Ice and Levi. She didn't think very much of that idea.

As she walked back out, she found Ice waiting for her. She glanced up, seeing the look on her face, which confirmed her own suspicions. "Michael wants me to stay with you."

Ice nodded. "You have a problem with that?"

"I have a problem in that I don't want to go anywhere but home so, yes."

"Things on the estate will blow up very quickly," Ice said. "As long as you're safe and sound, Michael can focus on what he's doing. That will make a huge difference in his ability to function at his peak levels."

"Bullshit."

Ice stared at her in surprise.

"Michael is dedicated and focused. He'll do the job."

"Of course he will." Ice gave Mercy a smile of approval. "But he cares about you deeply. The last thing we need is for him to be worried about someone coming after you in your apartment. If you stay with us for the next few days, he will know you're safe."

"Is it really that simple? How is it they would know where I live?"

"How did you get paid?"

Mercy frowned. "The usual route."

"Exactly. Once they have your numbers, they can easily track where you live."

Mercy realized she'd been foolish. She should've asked them to pay her in cash. It had never occurred to her. And Ice was correct. They would know where she lived. "Right. So, in that case, I guess I'm spending a few days with you."

Ice gave her a beaming smile. "It's not a hardship, I can

assure you."

Mercy chuckled. "No, but I'm not comfortable leaving Michael to go alone into the den of thieves either."

"He won't be. A big operation is being mounted right now. Michael is one tip of it."

"Good." She felt much better hearing that. She returned to the table and told Michael, "I still need my car."

He shook his head. "Don't worry about it right now. I'll take care of it. I have to get back to work by 7:30. So get moving."

She glared at him, then gave in gracefully, pulling her car keys from her purse, tossing them on the table in front of him. "You take care of yourself," she whispered.

He wrapped an arm around her and led her outside into the morning sun. The two stood, arms wrapped around each other. She tilted her head back so she could see his face, and with a brave smile and a sinking heart, she said, "So this is goodbye?"

He shook his head. "Hell no. I'll find you at Ice and Levi's place in a few days."

She studied his face, searching for the truth, realizing he meant what he said. Something settled deep inside her. She smiled and nodded. "Good."

As she turned to walk away, she caught a glint of something behind him. She reacted instinctively, throwing herself at him, knocking him off his feet. He fell to the sidewalk. The hard spitting sound split the air. She was tossed to the ground, then sideswiped by a vehicle. That was the last thing she knew before the lights turned off.

MICHAEL REACHED OUT a hand to keep Mercy down. He still wasn't sure what happened. But he'd heard the shot and was damned if she'd get another chance to save him again. "Mercy, stay down."

She didn't answer. She'd collapsed to the ground, her eyes closed.

And then he saw the blood welling up on her shoulder. He swore a steady blue streak as he realized she'd been hit.

He ripped the T-shirt off her shoulder, exposing the small bullet wound. Gently, he rolled her toward him so he could see if there was an exit wound as well. But there wasn't. Chances were, the bullet had lodged in her scapula. Now she would be at the emergency room, not home with Ice and Levi.

With Levi giving him cover, Michael picked her up and dashed to his vehicle. With Ice's assistance, they put pads on the wound and wrapped it as best they could to slow the bleeding. They propped her up with a seat belt around her. Jumping in behind the wheel, he pulled out of the parking lot at top speed with Mercy, leaving Ice and Levi to do what they could here at the crime scene.

None of them had seen any sign of the shooter. Levi had gone hunting but hadn't found him. The gunman may have disappeared, for now, but he couldn't hide forever. Michael would find him soon enough. In the meantime he took Mercy to the hospital, the nearest one only a few blocks away, so he didn't call for an ambulance. He'd get there much faster on his own.

He pulled into the Emergency parking lot of the hospital. Several EMTs milled around. Michael called them over, asking for help. When they saw Mercy's bloodstained shoulder, one man ran back for a gurney. Within minutes she was pushed toward the emergency room entrance. Michael followed closely behind.

She was taken straight through into a cubicle he wasn't allowed to enter. He stood outside the ER inner door, frustrated and angry, until a nurse told him, "We need your help with the paperwork."

"Of course." He followed her back to the intake desk. She lifted a package of baby wipes and motioned at his hands. He took several and wiped Mercy's blood from his hands.

"Let's begin with her name and address."

Trying to refocus, he gave the nurse the pertinent information.

"What happened?"

"She was shot in a restaurant parking lot, where we had breakfast."

And on it went. It took another ten minutes to fill out all the information. When it came to Mercy's insurance plan, he winced. "I'm not sure. I presume she has coverage through her employer. She's on leave right now."

The woman nodded. "She should wake up pretty soon, and I'll ask her then."

He shook his head. "The bullet is still inside. They might have to do surgery."

"Let them do what they have to."

He understood that, but, as he stood there, shifting, waiting, then pacing, he kept looking back in the direction of the emergency room hallway where Mercy had been taken.

Ice could've taken out the bullet and fixed that wound.

Then there was her father, a doctor who owned a hospital—but in California, not Texas.

His mind raced with random thoughts.

Finally the nurse finished the paperwork, and Michael was told to take a seat. He walked to the waiting area and paced instead.

When the doctor came out, he motioned for Michael. "She's gone to surgery to retrieve the bullet from her shoulder blade. She should pull through just fine."

Michael nodded. "All bullet wounds must be reported. I do have a detective's name. Maybe you can report to him?" He grabbed his wallet and pulled out the detective's card and handed it to the doctor. "It's all related to the same case this detective is working on."

The doctor nodded and walked away, the card in his hand.

Michael pulled out his phone and sent the detective a text, updating him. Then he did the same with Levi.

He walked over to the waiting room for the surgical patients. He hoped they wouldn't take long, but, with any surgery, she would be staying overnight. As he sat down to wait, his phone rang. It was his boss, Bruce.

"Where are you?"

Michael winced, realizing he hadn't called in his absence to the estate. He quickly updated him, saying he was waiting for Mercy to come out of surgery. There was an odd silence in the background, and he could hear a vehicle engine starting up.

"Stay there, Michael. If you come in at noon, that would be good. Work on the front beds today."

Michael nodded. "That I can do."

He put the phone on the table beside him and stared at it. This was the first time the boss had ever called him. But then it was also the first time Michael hadn't shown up for work. As it went, this morning had been a bit of a bitch. If only Mercy hadn't knocked him out of the way. Yet, if she hadn't, he'd have taken the bullet in his chest, likely killing him.

He kept checking his phone, hoping Levi had news. No way in hell was Michael leaving until she came out of surgery. It was the least he could do. The other part of his brain warred with this common sense. *She's not even awake. She won't wake for hours yet. Go to work. Give her a call when you're done.*

He shook his head. "Hell no."

Chapter 18

MERCY SURFACED IN a haze of confusion and pain. She rolled over on the bed and cried out as a fiery hot lance slammed through her shoulder. Moaning in pain, she rolled back over. She came fully awake, gasping for breath. Her hand automatically reached for her shoulder.

Her fingers, instead of touching smooth skin, came up against gauze wrappings that seemed to cover half her chest. When she opened her eyes again, it was to see a white ceiling, white walls, and a white curtain around her bed. She groaned softly, closing her eyes again. She was in the hospital.

She searched her mind, figuring out what had happened. She remembered breakfast with Michael …

Instantly fear rose. If she was hurt, what about Michael?

She opened her eyes, struggled to a seated position and looked around. But only her bed was in the curtained area. She didn't know if he was here or not. "Michael?"

She contemplated leaving her bed but saw the tubes in her arms. Gently, she lay back down again, continuing to fit the puzzle pieces together in her mind.

When did it happen? She remembered meeting Levi and Ice, agreeing to stay with them for a few days. They'd left the restaurant, and she thought she'd seen something. She still didn't know why she jumped toward Michael, knocking him back, but she had. And that was all she remembered.

She studied the large bandage on her shoulder. Had she been hit by a car? But that scenario didn't work as the rest of her wasn't sore. Although she wasn't feeling great overall either. She felt like a pound of meat worked over with a mallet. Or maybe a loaf of bread that had gone through a heavy kneading. Everything ached. And her head was fuzzy.

Then she remembered the glint in the distance. She'd been shot. She must have been. She'd pushed Michael out of the way and taken the bullet herself. Damn.

Still, she was guessing. But with nobody here to clarify, she couldn't be sure. And no way would she prod and poke at her shoulder to find out what had gone on.

She noted the Call button by her bed, but who would she call other than Michael? The hospital's peace and quiet, relative safety, at least at this point in her life, was something to savor. Then a door opened. She wasn't sure if she was in a ward or in the emergency room. Footsteps walked toward her. She waited, peering through her lashes. A nurse came around, pulling open the curtain as she walked to Mercy's bed.

She took one look and smiled. "Waking up, are you? That's a good thing."

Mercy wasn't sure how she knew she'd been waking up, but she dropped the pretense and opened her eyes slowly. She glanced around to see she was in a private room. "What happened?" she whispered.

The nurse raised the bed a bit and then held out a large glass of water with a straw. Gratefully Mercy sucked down several big gulps of water, feeling the dryness in her throat ease.

"Try not to gulp or drink too much the first time"

Mercy slowed to taking small sips. When she was done, the nurse returned the cup to the table. "You were shot. But not to worry. The bullet lodged in your shoulder bone, and you had surgery to remove the bullet. That's probably why you feel like you were beaten up."

Mercy didn't know what to say, but the facts lined up with her memories. "Is Michael okay?"

"Is he your boyfriend?"

Mercy nodded.

The nurse said with a smile, "Then hopefully that's the caged tiger pacing outside, waiting for you to wake up. He's been trying to come in, but since he's not family, we can't let him in. You're gonna be here for at least a day or two, so just relax." The nurse went about checking Mercy's blood pressure, temperature, then wrote notes on her tablet.

Mercy watched her in silence. The last thing she wanted was to stay here, but at the same time, if she was safe, if Michael could confirm the nightmare was over, well, maybe it was a good idea. She had to stay somewhere.

And she really wanted to see Michael. "Can I see Michael now?"

The nurse glanced up, assessed her expression and then smiled. "I'll let him in, in a minute." She walked out.

Mercy hoped the tests were over. Her shoulder was really pounding. The nurse hadn't checked the bandage, but she could see fresh bright-red blood seeping through the gauze. She had no idea how long ago she'd had any painkillers.

Then the nurse returned with medication. Mercy smiled

in relief. "I was just thinking how much the pain was kicking in."

The nurse nodded. "I will take a quick peek at the wound after you take the painkillers."

Unfortunately not enough time had passed for the new dose of painkillers to kick in, and the pain was incredible as the bandage was gently removed from her shoulder, the wound cleaned and a new bandage put on. She was covered in sweat, her whole body shaky. The last thing she wanted to do was be social. Neither did she want Michael to see her like this. On the other hand she was rather desperate to see him. She'd love to be held in his arms even for a moment.

The nurse patted her hand gently and said, "I'll give you a few minutes, and then I'll let him in."

Mercy didn't know when the few minutes came because she was so busy dealing with the waves of pain that had overtaken her system. When she could, she took several deep breaths, pushing the throbbing back down.

When she opened her eyes, she saw Michael standing beside her. She gave him a small smile and said, "Given a choice, I think I'd rather have stayed with Levi and Ice."

He gave a chuckle and whispered, "No doubt. But instead you decided to be a hero."

She gave a small shake of her head. "I'm no hero."

He reached down to hold her hand. "I've got news for you. When you push somebody out of the line of fire and take the bullet instead, that very much makes you a hero." He gently rubbed his fingers along the back of her hand. "I guess in this case that makes you my hero."

She smiled. "No. You're one of the good guys who goes

out and saves the world."

"I *was* one of the good guys. It's not what I do anymore."

She opened her eyes fully and studied him. "But you could. It's who you are inside. To turn down Levi's job offer would be to deny an inherent part of who you are."

He studied her for a long moment and pulled up a visitor's chair to sit beside her. "You don't know me well enough to say that."

She stared at him. "Yes, I do." Her tone was irrefutable. "We've been over this. You might not like to think anybody understands who you are, but that doesn't mean people don't. Levi and I certainly understand. And he knows you better than I do."

He pursed his lips. "Levi knows *of* me, and I've known Ice for a while, but I can't say we're very good friends."

"Would you have a problem getting Levi to watch your back?"

He shook his head.

"Would you have a problem having Ice watch your back?"

Michael snorted. "I could place my life in both their hands and know they would do everything they could to keep me safe."

She smiled. "What else do you need to know?"

He sighed. "It would mean moving."

"But they're here in Houston, right?"

"I live a couple of hours away. They are a 45 minute drive away."

"Would it be a tough move?"

He frowned. "I don't want to live in the compound. I want to live on my own land."

"So sell yours and move someplace closer. Or don't sell yours and rent it out and buy another place. Or rent another place, or try the compound, whatever the hell that is."

"It's not that easy," he protested.

"Of course it's not that easy, but it's not that difficult either. It depends whether this is what you want to do with your life or not."

"It's what I used to do, but I walked away from it. I'm not sure I want to get back into it again."

"And that is a decision only you can make." She smiled. "It would be a shame if you hid your light."

He snorted. "What will you do? After you recover from your bullet wound? You have to call work and let them know."

She shrugged. "No, I don't. I was taking three weeks' leave, remember?"

"Of which you've used nine days. Are you ready to return to that same job? After what you've seen of the world? The other side of the world?" he asked.

She studied him for a long moment. "Maybe. It's not like it's a job I feel compelled to do. But it's a job, and I have to have one of those."

He nodded. "If I move to Levi's, I'd be closer to you."

"And that's a good thing. Right?" She eyed him intently. What was he getting at? She wanted him to do what was right for his sake, but she didn't want to lose him.

He settled back, dropping her hand, and crossed his arms over his chest.

She grinned. "As body language goes, that's distancing yourself from a touchy topic."

"I don't like discussing those things," he muttered, glaring at her.

At that she laughed out loud. "Nobody asked you to discuss anything. It requires a simple yes or no answer."

He glared at her for a long moment, and then said, "Yes."

Warmth flooded through her. "Good. Go. It won't affect our relationship. I live in Houston anyway." Her smile fell away. She eyed him intently. "But I think we're getting ahead of ourselves."

"One of the reasons why I'm good at what I do is because I like to plan ahead."

She stared at him in astonishment. "Planning ahead is one thing. Planning ahead for a relationship is not quite the same thing."

"I'm planning to spend time with you." He gave her a flat stare. "If you are interested."

"Yes." After a moment of silence she chuckled. "Listen to us. Neither one of us is particularly open."

He shrugged. "We're opening up as much as we need to. The rest of the stuff is extra."

"How about you get me out of here?" she asked with a teasing grin. "So we can continue this relationship journey in private."

He gave her a slow smile with a twinkle in his eyes. "I was hoping you could be released before nightfall. Maybe spend the night together, but according to the hospital, that won't happen."

She frowned at him. "Maybe we should get a second opinion," she suggested with hope.

He laughed. "Nope, not happening. Your health comes

first."

"Being held in your arms is as good for my soul as staying in the hospital is good for my body."

He gave her a startled look. "Now that's a nice thing to say."

She gave him a slow smile, adding, "I mean it too."

Then the door opened again, and a man with a white lab coat walked in. He glanced at the two of them and asked, "How is the patient doing?"

She smiled up at him. "Excellent. We're discussing whether I'd be allowed to leave today and spend the night with him watching over me."

The doctor shook his head. "Not after surgery. We must keep you at least overnight."

"Fine then." She settled back, seriously unimpressed with the cut-and-dried answer.

Their discussion continued for another moment about where she would go when she was released and that she'd need rehab for continuing care, unless her own doctor could provide that service.

Once the doctor left, she was tired again. She shook her head. "How can I be tired? I just woke up."

Michael smiled, reached over and gave her a kiss on her cheek. "Sleep, sweetie. Just sleep."

She gave him a sleepy smile, curled up, still holding his hand, and closed her eyes. She was asleep within seconds.

MICHAEL WAITED UNTIL he was sure she'd fallen asleep again. Then he grabbed his cell phone and stepped out into the hall. He quickly sent Levi a text, giving him an update. When the phone rang seconds later, he knew who it was.

"Get your head back in the game," Levi said. "We'll keep her safe. But you need to return and set this up."

Michael groaned. "I know. My boss, Bruce, is expecting me at noon."

"Well, guess what? You're late." Levi hung up.

He stared down at his phone and knew Levi was right. He *was* late. He made the call to Bruce to report in. "On my way."

"Good, the work is piling up," was his only response.

But at least Michael hadn't been fired. Back in Mercy's corner room, he wrote down a little note on the scratchpad and left it at her side. Then he walked outside, climbed into his truck and headed back to the estate. So much had happened and yet, not enough. He needed to play the game for a little longer.

He struggled to focus on the drive. He was worried about leaving Mercy behind even though he had received a text from Ice, confirming she was at Mercy's side. At least he could stop worrying about that now.

As he drove in through the gate, one of the security men held up a hand and waved. Michael waved back, parked in front of his apartment and went to work.

He grabbed the wheelbarrow and dove into the mundane chores of weeding and raking out the front beds. He didn't know exactly what he was to work on after this but figured Bruce would get a hold of Michael soon enough.

About twenty minutes later his boss walked over to where he worked. They talked about a few nonessential things, and then Bruce handed over a work list. "We've got more company coming, and the owner wants the cedars thinned out along the driveway."

Michael looked at the long line of cedars in surprise. "All of them?"

Bruce nodded. "He's contemplating pulling them all down so there is increased visibility down the driveway."

"That would be a shame. I'll take away all the deadwood. Cedars are notorious for being full of dead branches and leaves on the inside. It'll make a huge difference if I can get that cleaned up."

His boss nodded. "That's your focus for the rest of the day." And, on that note, he walked away.

Michael kept a vigilant yet, distant watch. Nobody approached him while he worked. It was slow, hot, dusty work. The cedars were full and hadn't been cleaned out since probably forever. He gently opened them up, gave them a shake, cleaned out all the crap, grabbed the blower and blasted out all the debris inside the trees.

Three hours had gone by, and he'd only worked on about nine trees out of least thirty along this stretch. He would be here all of tomorrow.

Working on the next cedar, he broke up a huge pile of deadwood to dispose of, needing the trailer to collect all the debris. Walking back to the utility truck, he hopped in and backed up to the trailer, hooked on, and then drove down the driveway.

As he came up against the cedars, he could hear shouts behind him. He hit the brakes, stopped, and hopped out. "What's the matter?" he called.

Two guards raced up to him. "You can't enter that area."

He stopped and stared at them in surprise. Then he glanced down the road and said, "Okay." He shrugged as if he didn't care. He motioned to all the pruning piles set in front of each of the cedars he'd cleaned out. "I was only going this far anyway, to collect the debris."

The men looked from him to the truck, then to the piles and nodded. "I'll leave two men here with you," he said. Then he slowly turned and walked about twenty-five feet away. He stared at Michael and warned, "Make sure you don't go past the cedars."

"Whatever you say." Michael grabbed the rake and loaded up the first pile.

The truck trailer was more than three-quarters full by the time he cleaned up his pruning efforts so far. He eyed the trailer's capacity and then decided he could add the pruning from another couple cedars. He'd rather do the least amount of dump trips as possible.

He went to the next cedar and got started. He ignored the two men standing at the side of the road. He was also surprised they'd made it so blatant. He was all for them to make a move. Rage at what they'd done to Mercy ate at him. He was in control, but if they gave him a reason to break cover …

He pruned two more cedars, swearing and cussing about the irritating branches, making him itch, causing a rash on his skin. He loaded it all up into the trailer, then grabbed the broom to clear some of the finer debris, but he couldn't do a whole lot with it because this was a gravel road. Sweeping up what he could onto a tarp, he loaded the last of it in the trailer, putting the tarp over the load in the trailer.

He tied it down and said, "I'm heading to the dump now. Anybody coming with me?"

The two men looked at each other, then Robert, who had gone with Michael the last time, said, "I'll go."

Walking around the truck, he hopped into the front passenger seat. Michael pointed ahead. "Can I go down that way and turn around?"

Robert shook his head. "Nope, not allowed. Back up."

Swearing under his breath, Michael twisted in the seat, reversed, and slowly drove the trailer down the road. He had lots of experience driving trucks and trailers but had hoped for a chance to go farther down and turn around. But of course they wouldn't let him. When he finally turned around, facing the right way, he headed toward the main gate and out. "Must be quite the company if this much work is being done to prepare for them."

"Doesn't matter if it is or not," Robert said. "It's none of your business."

"Fair enough," Michael said.

He drove in silence during the twenty-minute trip, taking longer due to the heavy traffic. When they got to the composting material area of the dump, Michael turned the truck around and backed it up to an edge of a huge hole. Once there, he opened the tailgate, jumped into the back of the trailer and raked. It was more of the hot, dusty work. It was a good thing he was well used to manual labor.

When he climbed into the truck cab, Robert hadn't moved. But he was on his phone. Michael drove back toward the estate. "Time for a cold beer," he said in a conversational tone.

Robert snorted, putting down his phone. "I'm not off duty for another few hours. No beer for me."

"I'll be *drinking* of you," Michael said with a laugh. "This was pretty hot and shitty work today. I'm looking forward to having one." He drove up to the front gate, but another truck pulled out right in front of him. He slammed on the brakes hard.

The other driver gave Michael the finger and drove out.

A black SUV with smoked windows. Great for privacy. Very suspicious. Under his breath, as part of the act, Michael muttered, "Asshole."

Robert snorted. "Are you kidding? Most of these guys are assholes."

A shout sounded from the far side.

Robert shook his head, pointing to the parking lot. "They're calling for me. I gotta go." He opened the door.

Before Michael had a chance to come to a complete stop, the guard was out and gone, racing to the other vehicles, already running. Robert bailed into the front seat of one, and they drove out of the estate parking lot at top speed. Michael slowly drove around to the back where he parked the utility truck. He pulled Robert's phone from between the seats, where it had jammed after Michael had hit the brakes, and pocketed it. He had a small window of time to go through Robert's cell before Michael had to stash it again in the vehicle. Once Robert realized his phone was missing, he'd be back here immediately to search the truck.

Michael raced inside and upstairs. Soon he was locked in. He didn't have the time but couldn't miss sweeping the apartment for more electronic devices. As soon as he was done, he copied over all Robert's Contacts to his own phone. Then Michael copied the history of texts. What he had to do was make sure there was no sign of his intrusiveness afterward.

Getting in with the password was easy. Instead of coming up with a unique swipe, Robert had used a simple swipe pattern. Michael had seen Robert do it several times when he rode in the vehicle, so that wasn't an issue. Now that Michael was in, he busily moved through dozens and dozens of conversations. While in progress, he hooked up his USB to his phone, downloading them as he continued to take photos. On his laptop he sent everything to Ice and Levi and the commander. He wasn't exactly sure what he had here, but he had to get copies of everything as fast as he could.

Heart pounding, racing against time, he kept going. *Snap, snap, snap.* Again and again and again until he had as much as he could. He went through a couple conversations in an email account and copied them. This guy had everything open on his phone. Realizing copying directly from the SIM card might be faster, Michael pulled out the card, inserted it in his laptop and copied everything. When done, he replaced the card in Robert's phone and continued through the text messages. Michael didn't know what kind of timeframe he had, but he kept checking the gates for when the vehicles returned.

Finally, he came to the end. He quickly raced to the utility truck, wiping the phone free of his fingerprints, and stashed the cell between the two seats where it had been earlier. Leaving the truck unlocked, he headed to his place, where he put on coffee. He'd prefer a beer, but no alcohol while on duty.

Only ten minutes later the vehicles ripped back onto the estate. Michael tried to keep an eye on what they were doing, but they had pulled around back, where they couldn't be seen. From Michael's bedroom window, he watched as Robert raced to the truck, opened the door, and checked inside. Michael watched a look of relief on his face when he found his cell phone. Robert quickly pocketed the phone with a surreptitious look and rejoined the crew heading toward the big house. Michael had a pretty good idea that Robert wouldn't let anybody know he'd let his phone out of his sight. Now Michael had to hope what he had found on Robert's cell would break this murdering operation wide open.

Chapter 19

MERCY SMILED AT Ice when she returned with two cups of coffee.

"Levi just brought these for us."

Mercy chuckled. "Must be nice to have such an attentive man."

Ice gave her a wicked smile. "It's deadly nice. I highly recommend it."

Mercy shrugged, blushing slightly. "Maybe. We'll see."

Ice laughed. "Michael is a good guy. He was hell on wheels in the military."

Mercy nodded smiling at her initial assessment that she could see him in the military. "He is. He seems to be a little lost too." She thought about what she'd just said and shook her head. "No, he *was* lost, but he's more found now than ever."

"That's an interesting statement."

"Whatever caused him to leave the military had him trying to find his way this last year. So whatever he's doing now, whoever called him in to do this, did him a big favor. He enjoys this kind of work."

"Because he's good at it."

Mercy nodded. "So very true."

"Hopefully we can convince him to work for us afterward."

"He's more concerned about not wanting or liking the move. He mentioned the fact that he's settled where he is and doesn't want to live on the compound."

"Both valid points." Ice thought about it and was quiet for a moment. "Some of our members live in town or on property close by. Not everyone needs to be on the compound."

"Good. Not sure he's convinced yet."

"We've got time to work on him."

Mercy relaxed, happy to be away from the estate, knowing other people were looking out for her, that people were still working on her sister's case. She couldn't bring her sister back, but it would be nice to have answers and justice for her. Mercy also felt better knowing her sister had had Sammy, even if only for a short time. Anna had looked so happy in the pictures.

Mercy was delighted she'd found someone for herself. Life came with so many uncertainties. For a while, she wanted a few certainties. Something she could count on. Like the sun rising and setting every day. She wanted to wake up and see Michael's face and have it be the last thing she saw before she closed her eyes for the night.

That might not happen for a while, but she knew she'd move with him in a heartbeat if he asked.

Like her sister, she had felt trapped by the family scenario growing up.

Her mother had been poor; she and Mercy had worked hard. While still in school, Mercy felt like she was on an endless slog to an uncertain and dark future. She'd been jealous when her sister broke free of that life. Mercy had imagined Anna's experience in so many ways. Throughout the years Mercy had hoped her sister was traveling the world, becoming a globe-trotting independent businesswoman. She'd cast her sister in many different scenarios.

Yet, the reality was more like Anna living on the streets and selling herself for her next fix, but Mercy had never let herself think that way for long. To find out that her sister had landed a job at the estate with hard but honest work and had found Sammy, a good man, made her heart smile. It was so damn sad to not have known her sister at the end.

Her phone rang a few minutes later. Ice walked to the table—out of Mercy's reach—and handed it to her. It was Michael. She smiled as she clicked it on. "Hey, sweetie. How you doing?"

The rumble of his warm laughter filled her with joy. "I'm checking in to see how you're doing."

A muffled thump came on the other end of the phone. "Michael? Michael, are you okay?"

Silence followed. Then she could hear the phone moving around. A strange voice came on and said, "He is safe, for the moment. But, if you don't show up soon, he won't be."

"Wait. Who is this?"

And the phone went dead in her hand.

MICHAEL WOKE UP briefly, his limbs tied together as he was dragged along the ground. His head hit several rocks and jostled. He tried to shake the cobwebs from his mind, but the back of his head was pounding, and he realized somebody had sneaked up behind him while on the phone and taken him out. He wanted to scream in rage. Was everybody on this estate corrupt?

Two other men walked over, one on each side of Michael, and each picked up an arm and carried him. Then they lifted him up and threw him in the back of a pickup bed. His whole body screamed in protest. His head swam, but, with great difficulty, he retained consciousness. He locked on the image of Mercy, his mind determined to stay awake. He managed it for all of five minutes, until a second blow cracked down against his skull. The world blacked out.

Chapter 20

"SOMEBODY JUST HIT Michael," Mercy cried.

Ice's eyebrows shot up as she grabbed her phone.

Mercy swung to the side of the bed and gripped the metal railing as the room narrowed to one white dot. "I don't give a damn if the room is swimming around me," she said in a fury. "I have to get to Michael." With a couple deep breaths, everything calmed enough so that she ripped the IVs from her arm and the tape off her wrists. She struggled to her feet and walked to the closet, opening both doors to see if anything was inside. It was empty. "Where are my clothes?"

"Easy. You're not going anywhere," Ice snapped.

Mercy turned on her, her fury finding a target. "They said they're gonna hurt Michael if I don't get there." She shook her head and wished she hadn't. "I have to go. They'll swap him for me. I have to help him if I can."

"You can barely stand," Ice said.

"Maybe, but if you drive me close enough, I can do the rest."

"No way in hell."

Mercy jutted out her chin. "And no way in hell I'm *not* going. Michael's done so much for me. I can't leave him in the lurch."

"None of us will leave him. A team's being mounted right now. We'll go in to rescue him."

"That's fine, but we're taking a chance with his life. They have to see me to know I'm there. They'd probably want to take me out at the same time as him. Like they did with my sister and Sammy. These assholes won't take no for an answer."

"It's too dangerous."

"I know. But we're well past the point of *too dangerous*," Mercy said with more force than she intended. "This has to happen, and it has to happen now." She motioned toward the bed. "Do something constructive. Find something for me to wear. Because I will get out of this hospital, even in this gown, with or without you."

Ice studied Mercy's expression for a long moment and then gave a clipped nod. She raced from the room. As soon as she was gone, Mercy leaned against the closet doors. "Better save that bravado for when you will really need it, girl."

She made her way to the bathroom, quickly washed her face, used the facilities, and then came back out. Ice returned with a bag.

"The only thing wearable is your underwear and jeans, and even those are bloody. I found a sweatshirt in the lost and found."

Pushing the pain back down where it belonged, Mercy dressed, her mind figuring out how to get into the estate. Could she count on her ability to drive? "My car is still at the estate, isn't it?"

"No, it's parked in the parking lot."

"Good. You can drive it up to a block away from the estate, then you can disappear, and I'll drive it in."

Ice didn't say a word. Mercy didn't know if that meant agreement or if Ice would completely derail the plan with some idea of her own. She understood Ice was very much like Michael, and this was what they did. But Mercy was the one called to save Michael, and nothing Ice might do would stop Mercy from going in and helping him out.

The doctor came in, protesting mightily. She shot him a hard, flat look and said, "Wouldn't it be nice if life were perfect, and I could stay in bed and heal. But someone will die if I don't show up. That makes this a nonnegotiable conversation."

And she walked past him. She didn't know how the insurance would work, and she didn't give a damn. She hit the button on the elevator, and, with Ice at her side, they dropped to the ground floor. Outside they walked toward her car with Ice leading the way. She got in on the passenger side and took several deep breaths.

When Ice got in, she started the car, then looked at her. "You gonna make it?"

Mercy shot her a look. "I *will* make it. I have to."

Ice drove out of the parking lot and headed toward the estate.

"WHO DID YOU send the information to?"

Pain slammed into his head as an open hand struck his face. Michael tried to grab at it as his consciousness reached out and brought him back to awareness. He opened his eyes and looked around. Four of the security guards surrounded him. Crates were stashed all around him. He was tied to a chair, and, from the looks of it, he was inside the damn cave again.

"What?" He knew he couldn't fake it for long. But he hadn't left any telltale marks on the phone, so he had no idea how they would've known.

"The information you took off Robert's phone."

"What information?"

"He left his phone in the truck."

Michael managed a confused look, which was easier now that his head had taken so many blows. "He did?"

"Yes, he did. And your fingerprints were on it."

Damn, he must've missed something. No. They were guessing. "I had to hit the brakes hard," he muttered. "His phone fell, so my hand must have touched it."

Silence followed. He tried to free his hands and then his legs and stopped. "What's this all about?"

"Betrayal," a new man with a cool voice said, entering the fray.

Michael turned his head to the side as Freeman neared.

"I've had more than enough betrayal in my life. I have an easy answer for now. I just take out those involved."

"I never betrayed you," Michael gasped. The pain in his head rang through his ears.

"Well, the men have grabbed your laptop, and Tim's going through Robert's phone. So we'll see about that."

With a sinking heart, Michael realized that, although he had deleted and hidden everything on his laptop, and had done his best to delete every trace of his activities on Robert's phone, any technology geek could probably recover it.

"Where's Robert?" Freeman asked in a hard voice.

The men pointed to the far side. Robert was on the ground, unconscious. Blood flowed under him.

"Did you kill him?" Michael asked in horror. Inside he could feel the anger surging through him. His hands were tied with some kind of bungee around the back. His feet were tied with something similar. Getting out would be easy. He needed some time alone. Something he doubted he would have.

"He's not dead yet, but he will be soon."

"For what? For forgetting his phone in the truck?"

"Yes, exactly."

Michael let his eyes drift closed, and his head fell to the side. At least Mercy was safely away from here.

"When's the bitch coming in?" Freeman asked.

The question sent shock waves through Michael's system.

"She should be on her way now. I expect to see her in another five to ten minutes." When his phone rang, the security guard pulled it out, checked the text message and said, "She's coming through the main gate now."

Freeman nodded.

His fury building, Michael watched Freeman. It was all Michael could do to keep his expression blank. His fingers went back to work on the knots. "Who?"

"Mercy. Or should I say Anna's sister?"

Shit. So he had figured it out. God damn it. He sucked back his panic. "Oh, my God, what do you want with her? She's already in the hospital. Isn't that bad enough?"

"The shot missed. Never do these things in public," Freeman said to the guards. "Another reason Robert is down and out. He had lots of opportunity to take care of both of you. But he couldn't. After taking care of the last two he lost his nerve. Became spineless." He motioned to the body beside the guards. "Make sure you get rid of that soon."

He turned toward the open doors. "When she comes, shoot them both and bury them somewhere deep. No more finding bodies in shallow graves, like the last two."

"Is that what you do? Shoot anybody in your way?" Michael called out.

"Absolutely. The place is full of bodies." Freeman laughed. "That's one of the advantages of having lots of property."

"People have families and friends who will surely come looking for their loved ones," Michael said in disbelief. It was too much to even contemplate. "You can't just keep killing people."

"A spat some years ago forced me to take out a few people. And then a few people came looking, but thankfully we haven't heard anything from them in a couple years. Until the bloody maids and landscape gardeners turned into spies." He shook his head. "You can't get good help anymore." At the sound of a vehicle arriving, Freeman froze.

Michael watched Freeman, seeing the look on his face. "Who's that?"

"None of your business."

Michael turned his head and watched as Mercy's car pulled into view. Mercy wasn't driving; Bruce was. The vehicle was driven all the way inside the cave. Michael realized they would get rid of her car too. He had no idea what cover story Freeman would give the cops. Still, to have two sisters disappear from the same place was surely too much evidence for anybody to ignore. That was, if the cops knew about it. And two detectives did.

Thankfully Ice and Levi also knew, and, if anybody else disappeared, Levi and Ice would make sure something happened so the truth would come out. He watched in pain as Mercy slowly got out. She was obviously still struggling from her injury.

She took one look at him and raced unsteadily toward him. She dropped to his side and placed her arms around him, her head up against his chest. And she slid a small pocketknife into his hand.

He smiled inside. "I wish you weren't here," he whispered.

"How could I stay away? It was the only way to keep you safe."

Another chair was dropped down beside her. "Sit."

She shot the man giving the orders a hard look but slowly sank into the chair. Only Michael saw the wave of relief cross her face as she sat down, clearly not strong enough to be on her feet yet.

"What did we ever do to you? I came to save his life," she cried softly. "Why are you doing this?"

"Because we have to, and you're both going to die. So too bad for you," one of the security guards said. "Things must be dealt with before they become bigger issues."

She closed her eyes and whispered, "No, you don't have to do this. Is everyone on this estate corrupt?"

"Most of us," he said cheerfully. "Not Martha. She's devoted to John and turns a blind eye."

"Dear God," Mercy whispered. "It boggles the mind."

"You want us to tie her up?" one of the guards asked Freeman.

She immediately cradled her shoulder and whispered, "Please don't. I'm still dealing with the bullet wound."

The man shook his head. "Don't bother with it. She's not going anywhere."

One of the guards walked to Mercy's car and drove it farther into the cave. The others gathered around Freeman, standing before the crates.

Michael watched Mercy studying their surroundings before zinging her gaze back to Michael, an eyebrow slightly raised. He gave her a grin as the knife in his hand cut the last of his bindings. With the men's backs to him, he bent and freed his feet. But that was only part of the answer. Next was to get Mercy out safely.

With his hands held behind him, yet free, he held the knife open but concealed.

Bruce spoke to two of the guards. "Take them to the back of the cave where that new section is opening up. We'll bury them deep in there."

Freeman studied the crates while his men took care of the dirty business of murdering people.

At one of the guard's hand motions, Mercy slowly made her way to her feet. "Please don't hurt me," she cried out softly.

The other man shrugged. He pointed toward the back of the cave. "Then walk on your own."

The third guard neared Michael, thinking maybe a two-man team should be on him.

Michael took one scrutinizing look, measuring the distances, the weapons the other men held, and realized his chances were pretty damn thin. As soon as he started to walk, they'd see his bindings were cut. He straightened in his chair on his own. As he caught sight of Freeman and Bruce walking farther away, Michael turned the knife in his hand and lunged, stabbing the closest guard directly in his throat. Michael's free hand reached for the dead man's handgun and fired at the second security guard. And then he spun and drove a bullet directly in the forehead of the third security guard, standing beside Mercy. It happened so fast, nobody had a chance to react.

Mercy and the guard dropped to the ground at the same time, and she whispered, "I'm fine. Go."

He bolted for cover as she lay down, pretending to be dead. With three of the security guards down and Freeman and Bruce pinned on the other side of the crates, Michael quickly took a position where he thought he could pop off some shots. He had no idea what hell Levi and Ice had planned aboveground, but he'd get the details later.

"Who are you, Michael?" Freeman asked. "Like hell you're a fucking landscape gardener."

Michael gave him a ferocious smile. "I'm a man who loves plants."

"Well, you've pulled your last weed." Freeman fired a bullet, hitting the crate right next to Michael's head.

The wood splintered, sending several tiny pieces deep into Michael's shoulder. He shifted positions and came up in time to see Bruce poke his head around, looking for a shot. Michael pulled the trigger and dropped the man where he stood. Now that evened the odds more to his liking. Four down, one to go. "Give it up, Freeman. You've killed your last employee."

Freeman laughed. "Like hell." Several bullets sprayed around Michael as Freeman disappeared deeper into the cave.

Michael realized Freeman had to have an escape hole in the back. Michael hadn't had a chance to explore this area fully. He quickly followed. He had to hope Mercy stayed safe on the ground.

In the back was nothing but darkness and shadows, plus scurrying movements from every critter on earth that could possibly live in a place like this. But with his ears trained on the man, Michael heard the sounds of Freeman continuing down the cave.

Michael followed silently. The hunter and the prey. But when he thought he had Freeman, the dirty politician crossed to the far side, swearing, and then went silent again. Michael realized Freeman's plans had gone awry. Michael recognized the problem himself. There had been a small landslide of rock, probably from the last explosion they'd used to carve out a new entrance. But instead of being accessible to the surface, it was full of crushed rock and fallen debris. He grinned, picked up his pace and quickly retraced his steps, keeping sight of Freeman, still looking for a way to come around and get in front of Michael.

Mercy's car sat between the two men.

Freeman studied the car and bolted for the driver's door. He slid behind the driver's seat, and the engine turned over, now in Reverse. Michael slid into the front on the passenger side and pressed his gun against Freeman's temple. "Shut it off right now."

Freeman looked at Michael with a grin, and he floored it. Driving backward, straight toward Mercy, who still lay on the ground.

"Stop it," Michael roared.

Freeman shook his head. "Like hell." And he gunned it to go faster.

Michael pulled the trigger and yanked the steering wheel to the side. The right front tire narrowly missed Mercy. The car smashed into the entrance corner a moment later, with Freeman's foot still heavy on the pedal.

His head bleeding, Michael sat for a moment, getting his bearings, fighting with the airbags. Then his door opened, and Mercy's face filled his gaze.

"Are you hurt?" she cried out.

"Are you an angel?"

With tears in her eyes, she whispered, "No, I'm not, but you're my hero."

He shook his head. "No, not me. That was my old life. I'm no longer hero material."

With a gentle touch, she stroked his cheek. "I've good news for you. Once a hero, always a hero. Especially my hero."

And she disappeared from view as his lights went out.

Chapter 21

MERCY OPENED HER eyes and stared at the hospital room. Had she dreamt it all? She had had such horrible nightmares that she didn't doubt this could be just a continuation. But an odd breathing pattern had her glancing sideways to see Michael in the bed beside her. She studied his face anxiously, seeing the white bandage around the top of his head. He had some bloodstains on his cheeks, but he was fully dressed and stretched out beside her. She reached out a hand but couldn't quite touch him.

"Whoa, careful there." Ice came around the corner of the bed. "When he wakes up, he'll get closer. But at the moment, he's out cold."

"I gather our side won?" Mercy asked.

Levi popped up behind Ice. "We did. We were too late to save Michael from several knocks on his head, but we got there in time to take out the last of the guards back at the mansion."

Mercy smiled. "Did we get everybody?"

"More or less. I wanted to question some of the men, but Michael appeared to have killed them," Levi said. "He does have a bit of a heavy hand."

"He needed to. It was him against all those bad guys."

Mercy let her eyes drift closed, relief and joy flowing through her at hearing it was over, and they would both survive. "I was so scared when I arrived."

"But you didn't let it stop you from doing what had to be done," Levi said quietly. "There is a lot to be said for that kind of grit."

She shook her head. "I didn't even have to think about it. All I wanted to do was save Michael."

A warm hand gathered hers up gently. She gasped to see Michael's eyes open, staring at her, his gentle smile just for her. "It's much appreciated, but I'd rather you stayed safe."

"Then who would give you the knife to cut your bindings?" she teased.

"Very smart, falling down and playing dead," he admitted. "I wasn't sure what exactly happened."

She grinned impishly. "I learned that trick on the school playground years ago."

He rolled over slightly and stared up at Levi and Ice. "I presume it's over?"

Levi nodded. "The commander wants to talk to you."

Michael's eyes drifted closed. "Later. Much later." Then his eyes opened again. "You better not leave me in this goddamn hospital, because I'm not staying overnight," he said in a hard voice.

"Nope, you're not," Ice said with a big grin. "That doesn't mean you'll be any happier where you're going, but we wouldn't leave you here."

Michael stared at her. "And where's that?" His voice was flat, monotone, as if he expected bad news.

"You and Mercy are both coming to our place to recuperate. It's close and safe. It'll give you a chance to take a look at the compound and meet the rest of the guys. Some of them are good friends of yours."

Michael's brows rose. "I don't need babysitting," he said in scorn.

"I wouldn't mind though," Mercy said, her voice betraying how tired she was. "I need a good night's sleep, like a week's worth."

Michael turned, and pain flashed across his features at the motion.

"See? You're not feeling perfect either."

He studied her gaze for a long moment. "Is that where you want to go?"

"If it's not the hospital and not the estate, and I'm with you, then it's perfect."

Michael squeezed her fingers gently again, then looked at Levi and Ice. "Both of us? Together?"

Levi wrapped an arm around Ice's shoulders. "I know there is no compromise on that count. Some things I can't fight against."

"And what's that?" Mercy asked, not quite understanding what he meant.

He gave her a smile, his gaze traveling between her and Michael and back to Ice, and he whispered, "Love."

Mercy squeezed Michael's fingers this time. "Glad to hear that. I don't want to be separated from him again."

"And you won't be," Michael said with a promise in his voice. "Never again."

With a smile she let her eyelids drop closed, knowing she'd found a whole new future for herself. She said goodbye to her sister and to Sammy, knowing she couldn't help them anymore. It was time to focus on her and Michael. And she couldn't wait.

Epilogue

TYSON SAT AT the compound's dining room table. He hadn't seen such an incredible collection of men and women in one place since he had left the military. He never expected to see them in the private sector.

Levi spoke up. "Everyone, this is Tyson Morgan. He and Jace Colley will be joining us."

Tyson glanced at Jace. And then both of them looked at Michael. He shrugged. "Hey, I said it's a good place to be. You've trusted me before. Trust me now."

"We wouldn't be here if we didn't."

Michael smiled. "Then take it easy and relax."

A beautiful woman pointed toward the coffeemaker on the sideboard. "You can help yourself."

Tyson gave her a bright smile. "Thank you."

She beamed at him. "Don't worry about these guys. Every one of them has a really ugly bark. But they only bite if you're the enemy."

Jace snickered. "Hopefully we're all on the same team here."

"We are now. But that doesn't mean the odd person can come through here who's not."

Then Stone's voice wafted through the intercom. "Vehicle

approaching."

Levi stood and looked out the window. "Good. She's early."

"Kai." Ice chuckled. "What did you expect? Kai has never been late for anything in her life."

Michael spoke up. "Kai? That's a very unusual name. I've only ever known one person with that name."

Jace and Tyson both looked at Levi. Cautiously Tyson asked, "The weapons expert?"

"She's private now. Working for one of the military defense companies. But, yes, she's coming here to discuss some additional training we're all going to do."

Tyson felt a stir of interest inside. Which was an improvement over everything else that had been just plain dead for so long. Ever since he had walked away from the military—his ideals shattered at the betrayal of a friend of his—he hadn't had anything to intrigue him. Even coming here hadn't been a decision on his own as much as it had been following Jace and Michael. Especially Michael, who had been a large part of it. If this place was good enough to bring *him* out of retirement, then maybe this was where Tyson belonged too.

Kai ... Well, he remembered her as a small dark-haired dynamo who could put a man in his place in seconds. Not just by her tone of voice since she was military all the way. Not one of the men would've crossed her. She held their respect and their admiration. And he knew how more than a few guys had said she took top spot in their wet dreams.

Tyson glanced at Michael and saw laughter in his expression. Mercy, Michael's partner, kissed him on the cheek. Michael wrapped an arm around her and tucked her up close.

They were new in town. Apparently they were purchasing land together, building a place right next to the compound. Not a bad idea. There was some confusion about Mercy's future, except for one part of it: she was firmly attached to Michael.

Tyson didn't know what that felt like. He'd been alone since forever. Well, since he'd lost his wife and child. It seemed like his life had taken a downward turn for so long that he didn't know which way was up anymore. He was putting one foot in front of the other, because that was what he needed to do. But his heart hadn't been in it for a long time.

He'd have been lost without Michael this last year.

The door burst open, and the same dark-haired dynamo that Tyson remembered well strode in, her grin flashing. "Good morning, all. Ready for some fun?"

Her gaze went from one to the other, almost mentally counting them off, adding names, judging and assessing. When she studied Tyson, she inclined her head gently and said, "Hello, Tyson. How are you doing?"

And an old memory jolted Tyson at how Kai had been his wife's best friend when they were just kids growing up. And the pain never seemed to end. He nodded. "I'm doing great. You?"

She raised her eyebrows, seeing his lie for what it was. "You aren't doing great. You are doing barely okay. You're still in survival mode." She rubbed her hands together. "And that's a good thing. Because I came here to kick somebody's ass. You're it."

This concludes Book 10 of Heroes for Hire:
Michael's Mercy.
This also concludes Book 3 of the Sleeper Seals Series.
Book 11 is available.

Find out who the Commander calls next. Make sure to pick up ALL the books in the Sleeper SEAL series. These can be read in any order and each stands alone.

Protecting Dakota by Susan Stoker
Slow Ride by Becky McGraw
Michael's Mercy by Dale Mayer
Saving Zola by Becca Jameson
Bachelor SEAL by Sharon Hamilton
Montana Rescue by Elle James
Thin Ice by Maryann Jordan
Grinch Reaper by Donna Michaels
All In by Lori Ryan
Broken SEAL by Geri Foster
Freedom Code by Elaine Levine
Flat Line by J.M. Madden

Tyson's Treasure:
Heroes for Hire, Book 11

Buy this book at your favorite vendor.

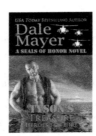

Heroes for Hire Series

Author's Note

Thanks for reading. By now many of you have read my explanation of how I love to see **Star Ratings.** The only catch is that we as authors have no idea what you think of a book if it's not reviewed. And yes, **every book in a series needs reviews**. All it takes is as little as two words: Fun Story. Yep, that's all. So, if you enjoyed reading, please take a second to let others know you enjoyed it.

For those of you who have not read a previous book and have no idea why we authors keep asking you as a reader to take a few minutes to leave even a two word review, here's more explanation of reviews in this crazy business.

Reviews (not just ratings) help authors qualify for advertising opportunities and help other readers make purchasing decisions. Without *triple digit* reviews, an author may miss out on valuable advertising opportunities. And with only "star ratings" the author has little chance of participating in certain promotions. Which means fewer sales offered to my favorite readers!

Another reason to take a minute and leave a review is that often a **few kind words left in a review can make a huge difference to an author and their muse.** Recently new to reviewing fans have left a few words after reading a similar letter and they were tonic to a tired muse! LOL Seriously. Star ratings simply do not have the same impact to thank or encourage an author when the writing gets tough.

So please consider taking a moment to write even a handful of words. Writing a review only takes a few minutes of your time. It doesn't have to be a lengthy book report, just a few words expressing what you enjoyed most about the story. Here are a few tips of how to leave a review.

Please continue to rate the books as you read, but take an extra moment and pop over to the review section and leave a few words too!

Most of all – **Thank you** for reading. I look forward to hearing from you.

I love to hear from readers, and you can contact me at my website: www.dalemayer.com or at my Facebook author page. To be informed of new releases and special offers, sign up for my newsletter or follow me on BookBub. And if you are interested in joining Dale Mayer's Fan Club, here is the Facebook sign up page.
facebook.com/groups/402384989872660

Cheers,
Dale Mayer

Your Free Book Awaits!

KILL OR BE KILLED

Part of an elite SEAL team, Mason takes on the dangerous jobs no one else wants to do – or can do. When he's on a mission, he's focused and dedicated. When he's not, he plays as hard as he fights.

Until he meets a woman he can't have but can't forget. Software developer, Tesla lost her brother in combat and has no intention of getting close to someone else in the military. Determined to save other US soldiers from a similar fate, she's created a program that could save lives. But other countries know about the program, and they won't stop until they get it – and get her.

Time is running out ... For her ... For him ... For them ...

DOWNLOAD a ***complimentary*** copy of MASON? Just tell me where to send it!

http://dalemayer.com/sealsmason/

Touched by Death

Adult RS/thriller

Get this book at your favorite vendor.

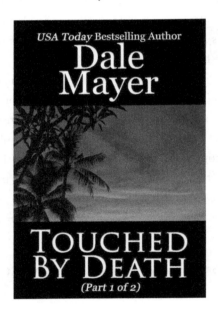

Death had touched anthropologist Jade Hansen in Haiti once before, costing her an unborn child and perhaps her very sanity.

A year later, determined to face her own issues, she returns to Haiti with a mortuary team to recover the bodies of an American family from a mass grave. Visiting his brother after the quake, independent contractor Dane Carter puts his life on hold to help the sleepy town of Jacmel rebuild. But he finds it hard to like his brother's pregnant wife or her family. He wants to go home, until he meets Jade – and realizes what's missing in his own life. When the mortuary team begins work, it's as if malevolence has been released from the earth. Instead of laying her ghosts to rest, Jade finds herself confronting death and terror again.

And the man who unexpectedly awakens her heart – is right in the middle of it all.

By Death Series

Touched by Death – Part 1

Touched by Death – Part 2

Touched by Death – Parts 1&2

Haunted by Death

Chilled by Death

By Death Books 1–3

Vampire in Denial

This is book 1 of the Family Blood Ties Saga

Get this book at your favorite vendor.

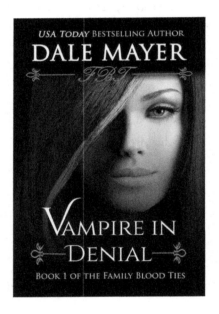

Blood doesn't just make her who she is...it also makes her what she is.

Like being a sixteen-year-old vampire isn't hard enough, Tessa's throwback human genes make her an outcast among her relatives. But try as she might, she can't get a handle on the vampire lifestyle and all the...blood.

Turning her back on the vamp world, she embraces the human teenage lifestyle—high school, peer pressure and finding a boyfriend. Jared manages to stir something in her blood. He's smart and fun and oh, so cute. But Tessa's dream of a having the perfect boyfriend turns into a nightmare when vampires attack the movie theatre and kidnap her date.

Once again, Tessa finds herself torn between the human world and the vampire one. Will blood own out? Can she make peace with who she is as well as what?

Warning: This book ends with a cliffhanger! Book 2 picks up where this book ends.

Family Blood Ties Series

Vampire in Denial

Vampire in Distress

Vampire in Design

Vampire in Deceit

Vampire in Defiance

Vampire in Conflict

Vampire in Chaos

Vampire in Crisis

Vampire in Control

Vampire in Charge

Family Blood Ties Set 1–3

Family Blood Ties Set 1–5

Family Blood Ties Set 4–6

Family Blood Ties Set 7–9

Sian's Solution – A Family Blood Ties Short Story

Broken Protocols

Get this book at your favorite vendor.

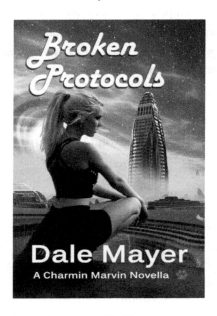

Dani's been through a year of hell...

Just as it's getting better, she's tossed forward through time with her orange Persian cat, Charmin Marvin, clutched in her arms. They're dropped into a few centuries into the future. There's nothing she can do to stop it, and it's impossible to go back.

And then it gets worse...

A year of government regulation is easing, and Levi Blackburn is feeling back in control. If he can keep his reckless brother in check, everything will be perfect. But while he's been protecting Milo from the government, Milo's been busy working on a present for him...

The present is Dani, only she comes with a snarky cat who suddenly starts talking...and doesn't know when to shut up.

In an age where breaking protocols have severe consequences, things go wrong, putting them all in danger...

Charmin Marvin Romantic Comedy Series

Broken Protocols

Broken Protocols 2

Broken Protocols 3

Broken Protocols 3.5

Broken Protocols 1-3

About the Author

Dale Mayer is a USA Today bestselling author best known for her Psychic Visions and Family Blood Ties series. Her contemporary romances are raw and full of passion and emotion (Second Chances, SKIN), her thrillers will keep you guessing (By Death series), and her romantic comedies will keep you giggling (It's a Dog's Life and Charmin Marvin Romantic Comedy series).

She honors the stories that come to her – and some of them are crazy and break all the rules and cross multiple genres!

To go with her fiction, she also writes nonfiction in many different fields with books available on resume writing, companion gardening and the US mortgage system. She has recently published her Career Essentials Series. All her books are available in print and ebook format.

Connect with Dale Mayer Online

Dale's Website – www.dalemayer.com
Twitter – @DaleMayer
Facebook – facebook.com/DaleMayer.author
BookBub – bookbub.com/authors/dale-mayer

Also by Dale Mayer

Published Adult Books:

Psychic Vision Series

Tuesday's Child

Hide'n Go Seek

Maddy's Floor

Garden of Sorrow

Knock, Knock...

Rare Find

Eyes to the Soul

Now You See Her

Shattered

Into the Abyss

Seeds of Malice

Eye of the Falcon

Psychic Visions Books 1–3

Psychic Visions Books 4–6

Psychic Visions Books 7–9

By Death Series

Touched by Death – Part 1

Touched by Death – Part 2

Touched by Death – Parts 1&2

Haunted by Death

Chilled by Death

By Death Books 1–3

Second Chances...at Love Series

Second Chances – Part 1

Second Chances – Part 2

Second Chances – complete book (Parts 1 & 2)

Charmin Marvin Romantic Comedy Series

Broken Protocols

Broken Protocols 2

Broken Protocols 3

Broken Protocols 3.5

Broken Protocols 1-3

Broken and... Mending

Skin

Scars

Scales (of Justice)

Broken but... Mending 1-3

Glory

Genesis

Tori

Celeste

Glory Trilogy

Biker Blues

Biker Blues: Morgan, Part 1

Biker Blues: Morgan, Part 2

Biker Blues: Morgan, Part 3

Biker Baby Blues: Morgan, Part 4

Biker Blues: Morgan, Full Set

Biker Blues: Salvation, Part 1

Biker Blues: Salvation, Part 2

Biker Blues: Salvation, Part 3

Biker Blues: Salvation, Full Set

SEALs of Honor

Mason: SEALs of Honor, Book 1

Hawk: SEALs of Honor, Book 2

Dane: SEALs of Honor, Book 3

Swede: SEALs of Honor, Book 4

Shadow: SEALs of Honor, Book 5

Cooper: SEALs of Honor, Book 6

Markus: SEALs of Honor, Book 7

Evan: SEALs of Honor, Book 8

Mason's Wish: SEALs of Honor, Book 9

Chase: SEALs of Honor, Book 10

Brett: SEALs of Honor, Book 11

Devlin: SEALs of Honor, Book 12

Easton: SEALs of Honor, Book 13

Ryder: SEALs of Honor, Book 14

SEALs of Honor, Books 1–3

SEALs of Honor, Books 4–6

SEALs of Honor, Books 7–10

Heroes for Hire

Levi's Legend: Heroes for Hire, Book 1

Stone's Surrender: Heroes for Hire, Book 2

Merk's Mistake: Heroes for Hire, Book 3

Rhodes's Reward: Heroes for Hire, Book 4

Flynn's Firecracker: Heroes for Hire, Book 5

Logan's Light: Heroes for Hire, Book 6

Harrison's Heart: Heroes for Hire, Book 7

Saul's Sweetheart: Heroes for Hire, Book 8

Dakota's Delight: Heroes for Hire, Book 9

Michael's Mercy: Heroes for Hire, Book 10

Tyson's Treasure: Heroes for Hire, Book 11

Jace's Jewel: Heroes for Hire, Book 12

Heroes for Hire, Books 1–3

Heroes for Hire, Books 4–6

Heroes for Hire, Books 7–9

Collections

Dare to Be You…

Dare to Love…

Dare to be Strong…

RomanceX3

Standalone Novellas

It's a Dog's Life

Riana's Revenge

Published Young Adult Books:

Family Blood Ties Series

Vampire in Denial

Vampire in Distress

Vampire in Design

Vampire in Deceit

Vampire in Defiance

Vampire in Conflict

Vampire in Chaos

Vampire in Crisis

Vampire in Control

Vampire in Charge

Family Blood Ties Set 1–3

Family Blood Ties Set 1–5

Family Blood Ties Set 4–6

Family Blood Ties Set 7–9

Sian's Solution – A Family Blood Ties Short Story

Design series

Dangerous Designs

Deadly Designs

Darkest Designs

Design Series Trilogy

Standalone

In Cassie's Corner

Gem Stone (a Gemma Stone Mystery)

Time Thieves

Published Non-Fiction Books:

Career Essentials

Career Essentials: The Résumé

Career Essentials: The Cover Letter

Career Essentials: The Interview

Career Essentials: 3 in 1

Made in the USA
Middletown, DE
16 February 2021